The Mind Game

Happy Reading!

Kelsie MacKenzie

11/11/25

This is a work of fiction. Names, characters, places, and any incidents either are the product of the author's imagination or are used fictitiously. Any resemblance to actual persons, living or dead, events, or locales is entirely coincidental. I would not use any of fictional works based on the above.

Copyright © Kelsie MacKenzie 2025

All rights reserved. No part of this book shall be copied in any way, which includes photocopying, recording, taping without the publisher's permission. Contact the publisher for permission to use any information in the book. Without permission by the publisher, with exception of copyright law, you may not use any part of this book for noncommercial use. To contact the publisher, email permission requests to:

Email: kelsie.mackenzie1212@hotmail.com

IBSN: 9798316064762 (paperback)

The

Mind

Game

Book *One*

Kelsie MacKenzie

This book is dedicated to my mom,

Who has always believed in me!

Trigger Warnings

Please Read!!

If there are any factors listed below or anything that I have missed that might make you feel uncomfortable or cause any mental health concerns, then I would advise you not to read this book. If you do read this book and if it does affect you in any way that may concern you and your mental health, please seek medical attention!

1. Domestic Violence
2. Mention of Suicide
3. Mention and Action of Abuse
4. Attempted Murder
5. Description of Murder of a Family Member
6. Attempted Rape
7. Mention of a Stalker
8. Alcohol Use

Table of Contents

Title Page

Dedication

Trigger Warnings

Table of Contents

    Prologue

    Chapter One

    Chapter Two

    Chapter Three

    Chapter Four

    Chapter Five

    Chapter Six

    Chapter Seven

    Chapter Eight

    Chapter Nine

    Chapter Ten

    Chapter Eleven

    Chapter Twelve

    Chapter Thirteen

Chapter Fourteen

Chapter Fifteen

Chapter Sixteen

Chapter Seventeen

Chapter Eighteen

Chapter Nineteen

Chapter Twenty

Chapter Twenty-One

Chapter Twenty-Two

Chapter Twenty-Three

Chapter Twenty-Four

Chapter Twenty-Five

Chapter Twenty-Six

Chapter Twenty-Seven

Chapter Twenty-Eight

Chapter Twenty-Nine

Chapter Thirty

Chapter Thirty-One

Chapter Thirty-Two

Chapter Thirty-Three

Chapter Thirty-Four

Epilogue

Prologue

Operator: 9-1-1, What's your emergency?

Woman in hysterics: My stalker is here, but I don't know where!

Operator: Okay. What's your name and address?

Woman: Linda Walker. 1256 Lincoln Road.

Operator: Thank you, Linda. How do you know it's a stalker?

Linda: He always texts me and follows me wherever I go. I know he's here because he texted me that he was coming for me! Please…send someone! *Starts crying*

Operator: Okay. Okay. Someone is coming. Just stay on the phone with me. Where are you now?

Linda: In the kitchen. Hiding behind my island counter.

Operator: Are all the windows and doors locked?

Linda: Yes

Operator: Okay. How old are you?

Linda: I'm twenty-four. Oh god, I hear footsteps.

Operator: It's going to be okay. The police are five minutes out. Can you—

Linda screams: NO! NO! PLEASE DO— *gunshot*

Operator: Linda? Linda!?

Chapter One

Evelynn

I don't know why Linda died. I just spoke to her yesterday and then she was dead? I knew she had a stalker, but did he really take it this far? Why though? I just don't get it. She didn't do anything wrong. She didn't deserve this. I blame myself for this. I should have been there for her, like I was supposed to be. Then this wouldn't have happened. She would still be alive. She had called me to see if I would come over because she was having mental health issues, but I told her that I wasn't able to because I had a deadline for the book I was writing and since I put it off for so long, my publisher was being pushy about me getting the next few chapters done. So, with music playing in my ears and laptop in front of me, I was completely lost to the world.

We called and texted each other all the time. I looked at my phone this morning, finding it weird that I didn't get a morning text, like usual. I did try calling her, but it had gone straight to voicemail, so I just left a message. It wasn't until an hour later that I got the call from her other friend that I didn't realize that she had. Apparently, he was a cop, or so he said. What was weird though was that he didn't even give me his name. I was in shock at first, not hearing the rest of what he was saying, but when we hung up, I started bawling. I threw my phone at the wall and collapsed onto my knees, leaned forward and cried onto the floor.

I gave myself thirty minutes to cry and calm down, before I sat up and wiped my tears off my face. I needed to call Jeremy. He should know about this, since we were all best friends. I stood up and walked to where my phone had landed; picking it up and seeing that it didn't break. *Lucky me,* I thought as I found Jeremy's number and pushed the call button. It took a few rings, but he finally answered.

"Hey…What's up?" He sounded groggy, I must have woken him up. All I did was start sobbing on the phone. *So much for the thirty minutes.* I didn't know how I was going to manage to get the words out, but I had to.

"Woah. Woah. What happened?" He sounded more alert and concerned now.

"Linda…she's…dead…" I said in between breaths. I felt like one of my panic attacks was surfacing. I needed one of my anxiety pills. There was a moment of silence.

"Shit…" was all Jeremy could say.

"Can you come over?" I asked, starting to hyperventilate. I haven't had a panic attack in a month. When my dad died a year ago, I was diagnosed with generalized anxiety, panic disorder, and PTSD. Then soon after it was severe depression, which branched into psychosis; also known as psychotic disorder. I was so messed up because all I had was my dad; he was my everything and I watched him get stabbed repeatedly. Twenty-four stab wounds, they said he had. We were out having dinner and suddenly, someone grabbed me as we were walking across the parking lot. My dad tried to get me from the guy who was holding me, but my dad was pulled away and that's when the stabbing happened. I am still haunted by the intrusive thinking and the memory of it happening, thinking that if I had tried harder, I could have saved him. I take meds for my mental health, and I stay grounded in other ways as well like meditation and yoga. Sometimes though, the dark likes to creep in. "Please?" I asked. "I just don't want to be alone," I managed to get out.

"Yeah," he responded, as I heard him quickly getting out of bed. "Take an anxiety pill and I'll be there in fifteen minutes." He then hung up, but two seconds later, he called me back. "Bye," he said.

"Bye," I replied, with a soft and staggered laugh. This time I hung up the phone and slid it into my pocket. Jeremy knew I had anxiety about people not saying bye. I would obsess about it because I wouldn't know if something happened to them or not. I couldn't say goodbye to my dad when he died because the guy who was holding me wouldn't let me go until my dad let out his last breath. Now, I needed everyone (in-person or not in-person) to say bye, so I can say that back to them; so, I felt like I had closure. It may be a weird quirk to have, but it was important to me.

I, clumsily, walked out of my bedroom, using every surface I could to keep me upright, like a baby deer when they first started walking, but eventually I made it to the bathroom. When I flicked on the light, I noticed that on my sink, my red lipstick was laying out and it was open. I glanced around my decent sized bathroom with a bit of confusion, but then I noticed the mirror…

You're

Next

I quickly backed out of the bathroom and hit the wall that was across from it, knocking down a picture or two. I slid down to the floor and my panic attack got worse. I couldn't breathe, and I started scratching my left arm. My panic scratches only came in really bad episodes like this one.

"Evelynn!" I heard my name being called and then footsteps running up the stairs, followed by Jeremy kneeling next to me.

"Fuck…this one is bad…" he said, referring to my panic attack. He grabbed my hand softly and moved it away from my arm, showing a big red mark with some open and slightly bleeding scratches. "I thought you were going to take an anxiety pill," he said. All I could manage to do was point towards the bathroom. He looked where I was pointing, stood up, and walked in. "Fuck…" I heard him sigh, as he said the word. He rummaged through some things and then I heard the water running. A few moments later, he came back out.

"Here," he said, handing me my pill and a small glass of water. I tossed the pill in my mouth and swallowed it with the water. He sat down next to me and pulled me into his arms, trying to comfort me until the medication kicked in. It took about thirty long minutes, but I had finally calmed down. We sat there in silence for another moment, before I moved away from him and sat up straight.

"We need to get the police involved," I said, after I cleared my throat. I leaned my head back against the wall and sighed. "Why me? It's bad enough that Linda died because of this fucker and now he wants me? What the hell did she do to deserve death?" Jeremy sat there listening as a million questions came to surface, one after another. "And why me? I barely leave the fucking house." After my dad died, I didn't go out much, unless I really needed to be somewhere or if I needed something from the store. Jeremy had offered to do the shopping for me, but it usually ended up with both of us going. Jeremy had always insisted. We were just close friends with nothing more attached to it, but he was kind of ruining my recovery with my therapist, but it was nice having the company, even on the bad days. My therapist was okay with Jeremy coming with me to places at the beginning, but I was supposed to be going out on my own by now, Jeremy just wouldn't let me. No matter how much I would talk to him about it.

"It will be okay," he said. "Let's just call the police and we will figure this out, okay?" I nodded and pulled out my phone, dialing the local police station.

Chapter Two

Lockwood

It was 10:45 am when we got the call that a female named Evelynn Matthews found a message on her bathroom mirror saying, 'You're Next'. At first, I wasn't going to bother with it because it could have been some sort of prank, but then I was told that she was friends with Linda Walker. The 24-year-old female that was murdered just last night. I quickly said that I would go to Miss Matthews's house to get more information. When I was given the address, I stopped short and looked at the sergeant, who told us about the crime.

"You're shitting me..."

***

My partner, Detective Kane Wilder, and I pulled up to Miss Matthews's house at around 11:30 am. It was a decent house. White with light blue curtains, from what I could see, two stories, a nice wrap-around porch with two chairs and a swing chair. Just your standard house in the city of Ark Hollow. The police officers were already here to go over the events, but once we had read the incident report, I knew we had to go check it out ourselves.

"Well look at that..." Wilder said as he pointed towards a house that was across the street and a few houses down, "Looks like Miss Matthews lives pretty close to Miss Walker." I looked at where he was pointing and sure enough, there sat Miss Walker's house.

"With being that close to her friend's house you would think that she would have heard the gunshot or seen the collection of police cars in front of the house," I thought out loud, looking over at Wilder. All he did was shrug, get out of the car, and head towards the house, with me following his actions.

Once we were at the door, we looked at each other and then I knocked. A moment or two later, the door opened and there stood a female that looked to be in her early 20s. She had beautiful, thick, long, medium brown hair. Her light blue, doe-like eyes stared at me for a fleeting second, before she looked away. She seemed to have this rose beige look to her skin and she may be the height of 5'5" I briefly looked down at her mouth, full lips and all I wanted to do was – I felt a jab in the arm and looked up at Wilder, realizing that I must look like an ass for just staring. I cleared my throat and grabbed my badge, showing my credentials, Wilder did as well.

"Umm... I'm Detective Bradley Lockwood and this is Detective Kane Wilder," I introduced us as we put our badges away. "You must be Miss Matthews..." I glanced behind her, seeing there was a blonde male. "Oh... I'm sorry... I didn't know you were married..." I tried to hide my disappointment. "Mrs. Matthews then?" What was wrong with me? I didn't even know her. I certainly had never seen her before. So, why am I feeling disappointed? I noticed her give me a confused look and then look behind her.

"Oh! No… we aren't married. He is just my best friend," she explained, looking at me with shock. I didn't miss the fact that he had the look of heartbreak written all over his face when she said that. I, of course, felt a sense of relief. "And please… just call me Evelynn," she said with a smile. *I'm gonna be done for,* I thought. I heard Wilder clear his throat.

"Can we come in to go over some things?" he asked, with his naturally deep voice.

He was fairly attractive, 6'3", well built, and had chestnut skin, brown eyes (the ones that make women "swoon" apparently), his hair is short enough that it was close to being bald, and a mustache to match it. Then there was me who was 6'2", short, brown wavy hair. A toned body underneath my clothes. I also have a short full beard and deep brown eyes.

"Yes, of course! Come in," she said quickly while moving to the side and letting us in. I scanned the house, seeing that it was well decorated. There were photos on the walls, some plants, the walls were off white, and I could see there was a fireplace in the open living room. There was wood flooring, but a giant carpet covered some of the floor in the living room. There was also a big L-shaped couch and a loveseat, that was white leather and then I noticed the big tv hanging on the wall, above the fireplace. What did she do for a living? I then looked back at

Evelynn, which caused my heart to skip a beat, especially when she looked at me. Is she blushing? I assumed she was because she had quickly looked away. The blonde male was being curiously quiet, not to mention he had the look of anger on his face. *What was his deal?*

"Do you guys want anything to drink?" she asked, looking between me and Wilder. "I have bottles of water, coffee, lemonade, and coke." She had her thinking face on as she listed the drink options. I couldn't help but internally chuckle. She was cute with that expression on her face.

"Water is fine with me," I responded with a small smile. She then turned her attention to Wilder.

"Coffee would be great," he said. "Have a long day ahead of me, so I need all the fuel I can get!" he said jokingly as he received a small laugh from her.

"I hope instant coffee will be okay… I haven't had the chance to make—" She was then interrupted by her companion, which irked me. I hated people who interrupted others.

"I already made a pot," he said, looking at Evelynn. She looked back at him surprised.

"Well, thank you, Jeremy. I'll be right back," she said, giving us the most heavenly smile. I almost went down on my knees to worship her. She then turned around and headed down the hall, disappearing into what I assumed was the kitchen.

I put my attention back onto the blonde male, apparently known as Jeremy. Compared to me and Wilder, he seemed to have a height of 5'11". Upon closer view, I could see that his hair was dirtier blonde. He had a short, full beard like mine, but a little thicker. He had green eyes and from what I could tell, he seemed to have a toned body.

"So, Jeremy… how long have you known Evelynn?" I asked, getting the ball rolling so we could start the investigation. There just seemed something off about him.

"About a year and a half," he responded, glancing at me, but not exactly looking at me. He seemed nervous, but that could be because he was worried about Evelynn with what had happened.

"Did you know Linda Walker from down the street?" I questioned, watching his body language; seeing how he would react to the question. He stayed silent for a while but then answered.

"Yeah, I knew her." I noticed his hand started fidgeting. I was about to comment about it, but Evelynn came towards us from down the hall. She had two bottles of water, a coke, and Wilder's coffee.

"Here… let me help you," I said, as she approached us. I grabbed the two bottles of water from her arms.

"Thank you," she said, smiling at me. *That damn smile.* She went to give Wilder his coffee before realization showed on her face. "I'm so sorry! I forgot to ask if you needed cream or sugar…"

Wilder smiled and took the coffee mug from her. "Black is fine," he replied as he took a sip. What's funny is that... Wilder didn't care for black coffee.

"Who does this belong to?" I asked, holding up one of the bottles of water.

"It goes to Jeremy," she said, taking the water from me. Our fingertips overlapped with each other, and I felt a spark, radiating through my body. I didn't think it would faze her, but surprisingly, she moved her hand slowly from mine and handed the water to Jeremy. *Wait... why did she move her hand slowly?*

"Shall we?" she said as she opened her can of coke and led us to the living room from the entryway. Wilder and I took the couch, while the other two took the loveseat. Evelynn sat sideways at the end of the loveseat, putting one leg underneath her and the other foot planted on the floor. Her elbow rested on the back of the love seat while her head rested on her hand. Jeremy sat close to Evelynn having splayed his arms on the back of the loveseat, which meant that one of his arms was behind her.

Claiming dominance. I looked at Evelynn who noticed me analyzing Jeremy's actions. She had an amused smile on her face, shaking her head softly and rolling her eyes. Was that because of his actions or mine? I let out an internal sigh, as I took out my memo notebook. *I need to keep it together. Focus.* I grabbed my pen and opened the notebook to the first page. I looked at Evelynn and was about to start, but Wilder beat me to it.

"You seem rather calm, considering everything that has happened..." Wilder said quizzically. I glanced over at him, then back over to Evelynn.

"She had to take one of her anxiety pills," Jeremy started to say, and my attention switched to him. "She had called me when she was having a panic attack. So, she asked me to come over and by the time I got here, it had gotten worse," Jeremy continued. "I went into the bathroom, saw what was written, and then gave her one of her pills," he finished. "That's why she is calm."

Defensive much? I looked back at Evelynn, "How come you didn't take one before you called him?" I asked with curiosity. Part of the job was based on getting all the details, but I was also a little concerned.

"She was—" I raised my hand towards Jeremy, stopping him from continuing to talk for Evelynn, which I found annoying

"I'm sure Evelynn has a voice and can answer the questions we ask *her*," I said, putting emphasis on her. That must not have sat well with him because he just glared at me, which I didn't give a flying fuck.

"Take a deep breath," I heard Wilder say, low enough for only me to hear. He could tell I was getting annoyed and if it would continue, it would cause me to get angrier than I already was, and no one would want that. "Remember the Jaxon incident..."

***

Captain leaned towards me, "Lockwood... Go to the back and see if you can get in." I nodded and headed towards the back.

We were here because Trey Jaxon was called in by a neighbor because they heard screaming from both Trey and a female that went by the name Lilia Rosenthal. There was also a gun that went off when we approached the house. We were also told that the couple always had issues and that the police force had been called many times because of worry for the female. We did remember this, but this time was different. There was even a gunshot before we were called.

Once I made it to the back, I checked the back door to see if it was unlocked, but of course it wasn't. I checked all the windows and luckily one was unlocked. I slowly opened the window and looked in to see if there was going to be something in front of the window, but there wasn't. I slowly and silently entered through the window, seeing that I was in an office space. I was going against protocol by just sneaking in, but I wasn't going to let things get more out of control than it already had.

I tried being quiet, but almost all of the floor would creak, making me wince and listen for any indication of them hearing me. Soon enough, I made it to the door and slowly opened it; being grateful that it didn't make any sound. I walked into the hallway and started walking down it, *making a few creaks, but not as bad as the office. I soon made it to the entrance of the living room and to my surprise they were facing towards me. So, they **did** hear me. What I saw made my blood start to boil. Lilia was covered in bruises, and her lip was busted. What threw me over the top was that Jaxon was holding a gun to her head. I quickly whipped out my gun and pointed it at Jaxon, because he was stupid enough to not shield himself.*

"Let her go Jaxon..." I said calmly but demandingly. "Let's make it easier for both of us," I said as I slowly crept towards them.

"Stay there! I'll shoot her!" Jaxon yelled and it was obvious he was drunk, by the way he was swaying and slurring his words. I halted to a stop, but didn't lower my gun.

"Jaxon... I'm warning you... Let her go," I said in a deeper tone.

"Throw your gun away from you!" he demanded. I laughed internally at him thinking he could tell me what to do.

"I'm not going to do that until you let her go." I hated when people made me sound like a broken record. I saw that he was slowly pushing on the trigger, threatening to kill Lilia. I took a step forward before I heard a gunshot and I was on the ground, clutching the front of my right shoulder. Then I heard a second gunshot and watched as Lilia fell to the ground. I quickly grabbed my gun and shot Jaxon in the stomach, as I was standing back up.

I saw that he was obviously still alive, because even though the stomach was a fatal part of the body, it was a slow death. I quickly went over to Lilia, while keeping an eye on Jaxon. When I approached her body there was no mistake that she was dead since she was shot in the head. Anger didn't even cut it with how pissed off I was.

I charged at Jaxon and kicked his gun away, then straddled his body, using my knees to hold his arms down. Before I knew it, I started punching him in the face, repeatedly, to the point of him being unrecognizable.

Suddenly, I heard yelling and motion, then Wilder grabbed me and pulled me away from Jaxon's body.

***

I nodded and took a deep breath in, then slowly let it out. I put my attention back to Evelynn. When I did that, it felt like I became calmer. I saw the look of confusion on both Evelynn and Jeremy's faces, but I quickly continued the interview.

"Evelynn…" was all I said, wanting her to answer the question. My heart skipped a beat when she placed her doe-eyes on me.

"I was going to after talking to Jeremy," she began, placing her coke on the table that was next to the loveseat. "I made my way to the bathroom from my bedroom and once I entered, I noticed the writing on the mirror." She was getting anxious again. "I quickly backed out, hit the wall and my panic attack got worse." Even though her sleeves were down; she was pulling at them anyway. I noticed her breathing getting heavier and I looked at Jeremy.

"Jeremy… would you get me another anxiety pill please?" she asked, turning her head towards him. He looked at me hard before he stood up.

"Do you still have some in the kitchen?" he asked, looking down at Evelynn.

"Yeah. Same spot as usual," she replied to him. He nodded and headed to the kitchen. She then removed a Ziplock bag out of her jeans pocket and held it up to us, showing us that there were pills inside. "Okay… he's gone…" she said with relief. "Now, we can talk easier without him taking control…" She moved her legs into the ankle crossing position, looking more relaxed. "We have five… maybe ten minutes before he gives up looking and comes back in here." Wilder and I looked surprised and glanced at each other.

"So, you're not having —" She chipped in before I could finish, but I let it slide.

"No… that was just a ruse." She winked, giving us a smile. "Now hurry and ask your questions," she urged us.

"Is he always this controlling?" I asked, resting my arms on my knees and looking at her intently. If he was controlling that means, there could be some sort of abuse. Now, I really wanted to see her arm. This would make him our prime suspect for this now Evelynn case and I would think that Wilder knew it too.

"I don't let it get to me… It's better that way." She said the last part in a softer voice, but I still picked it up. I was on the verge of going over to her, but Jeremy came back… earlier than expected. I watched as Evelynn quickly put the Ziplock bag back in her pocket.

"I think you need to restock your kitchen stash," he said to her, taking his spot on the loveseat next to her. "I found this lonely guy hiding in the cupboard." He held it out for her.

"Thank you, Jeremy," she said, taking it from him and swallowing the pill with her coke, even though it wasn't needed. There didn't seem like there was tension between the two, so is there actually abuse? There had to be. She wouldn't have wanted him to leave the room and there was that comment she had made in a soft voice, not necessarily that she didn't want us to hear, but I still thought there had to be something more going on. Something just didn't sit well with me, and I needed to get out of there, before I did something that I would regret later. I heard Wilder sigh; he knew I was getting close to the point of no return.

"Can we see the bathroom mirror now?" Wilder asked, taking over the interview.

Chapter Three

Evelynn

  I really didn't want to go back into that bathroom. I didn't know when I would be able to. Someone, most likely Linda's stalker, had come into my house and besides writing that message on the mirror, who knows what else he did. Did he watch me sleep? Did he touch me? How could I even stay in this house? I didn't know where else to go though, definitely not at Jeremy's. I know he would offer, but I would just decline and say that I would be fine. Maybe I can ask for someone to watch outside my house? I'll ask when things are about to wrap up.

  We went up to the bathroom, but I stopped moving forward. I looked at the two detectives and I think they knew I wasn't going in there, because Detective Lockwood nodded and motioned Detective Wilder into the bathroom. Jeremy was beside me, holding my hand. I never wanted this kind of affection, but there was nothing I could do about it. When he gets mad, he tends to get violent with me, so I try to avoid it as much as possible.

  The detectives were only in there for a few seconds, before coming back out. They looked perplexed, and I didn't understand why. I walked over to them and investigated the bathroom, the writing was gone, the lipstick wasn't where I saw it before. None of it made sense. It was there!

"It's not there, Jeremy…" I said, looking at him.

"Evelynn… was there ever a message?" Detective Wilder asked. I spun around, looking at him in astonishment. I looked over at Detective Lockwood and saw that he was glaring at him. "Just answer the question," Wilder said sternly.

"Of course there was!" I exclaimed. Was that even an appropriate question? They didn't need to know that sort of information, in my opinion, the mental health of a person should not be questioned. I pointed at Jeremy. "He saw it, too!" When I didn't hear him say anything, I turned towards him. "Aren't you going to say anything?" I asked in frustration. He sighed and I knew that whatever came out of his mouth wasn't something I was going to like.

"I'm sorry… but I didn't see anything…" he confessed; guilt was plastered on his face. Lockwood gave Jeremy a suspicious look and I knew he remembered that Jeremy had said he *had* seen it, catching him in a lie.

"Are you fucking kidding me!?" I yelled. "You reacted to it!" I yelled, pushing him. I knew I was going to regret that later, but he couldn't just help me with this.

"I reacted the way I did because it wasn't there… I think you might be going through an episode again, Evie," he said softly, which earned him a slap in the face.

"Woah! Hey now!" Lockwood interjected because Wilder was in the process of coming to arrest me. He came over to me and lightly grabbed my arm, getting my attention.

"Do not bring that into this!" I shouted, trying to get at Jeremy again, but Lockwood didn't let me go. It was for the best though. I was going to be in enough trouble as it was, since I got aggressive towards Jeremy.

"Okay, Okay," Lockwood said, guiding me away from Jeremy. "Let's go into another room and talk. Where can we go?" he asked, looking at me with patient eyes. My heart skipped a beat, and I swear I could feel my cheeks get warmer as I looked back at him. "Breathe…" he mouthed, so the other two couldn't hear him. I exhaled, not even knowing I was holding my breath in the first place. *Well, that's embarrassing.*

"My room…" I replied breathlessly. Suddenly, my phone dinged twice, alerting me that I had a text. I looked down at my pocket and then looked at Lockwood, who gave me a nod in response. I pulled out my phone and opened the message app, but as soon as I saw the name, I dropped my phone in horror.

"No… No… This can't be happening," I said, putting my fingers in my hair. "Please… No…" I backed away from the phone, staring at it. I turned around and ran into my bedroom, slamming the door.

Why? Why now? I thought repeatedly, as they echoed inside my head, and I started to pace the room. Was Jeremy, right? Was I going through an episode right now? I swore that the writing was on the mirror and when I saw the text I got, I just freaked out and had to get away from everyone. It was short lived though, when I heard a knock.

Chapter Four

Lockwood

I watched Evelynn as she ran down the hall and into what I assumed to be her room; frantically at that. I looked down at her phone; it was lying face down. I looked over at Jeremy.

"Can you see what scared her?" I asked. "You have more of a right to do it... we need a warrant to check," I explained, making a gesture with my eyes, telling him to 'go ahead'. He looked at me, down at the phone, and then walked over to it. He seemed nervous to see whatever it was, but he bent down and picked it up. He turned the phone in his hands, so the screen was turned upwards and started punching the screen with his thumbs. After a few more screen taps, he sighed.

"There isn't anything there that would freak her out that bad. Not that I can see," he said as he held out the phone to me. I wouldn't take it though.

"I'm gonna go talk to her... get some more information from her," I said to them. "I also want to see if she is okay before I bombard her with questions." I then turned and started heading towards her room. I approached the door and knocked. "Evelynn... can I come in?" There was a moment of silence before she gave me the okay to enter. I opened her door and stepped in, closing it behind me.

As I glanced around the room, I saw that the walls were painted a light blue. Her bed wasn't a four post, rather it was a king-sized bed that was sitting on a wooden platform that had drawers. The bedding was white, but she had a light blue down blanket. All the furniture was white, but what caught my attention was two tall white bookshelves in the corner, standing side by side. They were set so they were up against separate walls but snugged together. They were filled with books, but I did notice there were piles of them next to each bookshelf. Next to one of the bookshelves there was a big window with a sitting nook.

I looked to where Evelynn was, and she was pacing. I wouldn't be surprised if she had been pacing before I came in. What would be freaking her out so much? Jeremy said there wasn't anything on there. I should have taken the phone and just not looked. I didn't totally believe him. Not with what I was witnessing now.

"Evelynn…" I said her name softly and slowly approached her; I didn't want to startle her. "Evelynn…" I said again, since she didn't respond the first time. She stopped pacing, which made me stop moving towards her. She stayed silent for a moment, before turning towards me.

"Was there actually anything on my phone?" she asked, looking at me and I could see she was crying. It was one of those cries that only a small amount of tears fell down the face, but based on how red her eyes were, she had been crying more than what I was seeing. "Was there anything on my phone?" she asked again.

"I don't know," I replied, looking back at her. Her eyes were still beautiful, even when red and puffy. I just wanted to wrap my arms around her, just so I could comfort her, but it would have been unprofessional. "Without a warrant, we can't look, and Jeremy said that nothing was on there... not that I believe him." I quickly said the last part, wanting to make sure that was clear to her.

"Of course he did," she scoffed, wiping her tears away. "He probably deleted it... in case you did look." She groaned and ran her fingers through her hair.

"What did *you* see?" I asked her, trying to do work and showing her care. I was in her corner of the ring, and she needed to feel like someone was.

"Why does it matter?" she asked, looking at me again. "There, *apparently*, wasn't anything on there, so I have nothing to back up what I had seen." There was something she wasn't telling me, and I needed to know what.

"What did Jeremy mean by episode?" I asked, hoping to not upset her even more. I need every single bit of information I could get for this investigation.

"I don't want to talk about it," she muttered, crossing her arms in front of her. There were many reasons why she would do that, and my guess was that she was anxious. This wasn't a topic she wanted to be open about, so I wasn't sure if I should push it, or leave it for now.

"Okay… we won't talk about it," I said, deciding just to leave it for now. "But we will have to talk about it eventually."

Chapter Five

Jeremy

I watched as Detective Asshole walked down the hall and went into Evelynn's room. I didn't like that at all. I wasn't expecting him to go after her. I thought he would want to talk to me more, to get information. She was in no state to talk, let alone talk to someone she didn't know. *She needs me right now,* I thought, but I didn't forget about her slapping me and pushing me. She wouldn't get away with that, but she needed comfort right now. Maybe, I shouldn't have brought up Evelynn's mental health, especially that part, but wouldn't it help the detectives in some way? That didn't matter right now. I needed to go to her.

"Does Evelynn have mental health concerns?" Detective Wilder asked, before I could start down the hall. I sighed and turned to him. There was no use in hiding it now.

"Yes, she does…" I answered with concern and a small nod. Just because I do what I do, it doesn't mean I don't care about her and that I don't love her. I care about her immensely and love her more than life itself, but when she does something wrong, she deserves the punishments that I give to her.

"We are going to need to know what she has…" Wilder said sternly. What was up with these detectives giving me such an attitude, especially that Lockwood guy. That detective has it out for me.

"It's not my right to say," I replied, nonchalantly, as I leaned on the wall. I could tell that it irked him, but that was pretty much the idea. Just because they were cops, doesn't mean they deserved respect.

"It's important for us to know, for the investigation," Wilder explained, as he crossed his arms. "We need to know everything that could help us," he said, looking at me dead on. *Now... Do I continue messing with him, or should I just get it out there?* When I noticed him continue to give me that stern look, I sighed and relented.

"Okay…okay…" I said, holding my hands up in defeat. "I'll tell you everything."

Chapter Six

Lockwood

I glanced at her arm, remembering her pulling down her sleeve. She was also giving signs of being abused, so for her safety, I needed to know. She was now sitting on her window seat, with her knees up and staring out her window. I sat down on her bed, with her permission, and we stayed silent for a couple minutes. I wanted her to be calm and in a good head space for when we started talking again.

"Evelynn," I said smoothly, getting her attention. When she slowly turned her head to look at me, I continued, "What happened to your left arm?" I asked with concern. She looked down at her covered arm, then back at me.

"Panic scratches," she replied with a sigh, looking back out the window. "I had found out that Linda died and that was when my panic attack started," she started to explain. "Then, when I saw the message on my bathroom mirror, my anxiety heightened even more, and then I started scratching," she finished, looking back at her arm. She pulled the sleeve back and I could see the big red marks, along with some open scratches. "It doesn't happen all the time… it's been a while since it last happened." She pulled her sleeve back down and gave me a sad smile, it was nearly heartbreaking. I looked at her and I needed to ask her about the suspected abuse.

"I'm going to ask a very hard question, but I need you to be honest with me," I said sternly. When I saw her nod, I looked right at her when I asked her the next question, "Is Jeremy abusing you?" Her eyes went wide as she looked at me. *Well, that answers my question,* I thought as I let out a quiet sigh. "What has he done to you?" I asked, trying to keep an even tone. I saw the gears turning as she debated on telling me or not.

"It doesn't matter... I always deserve it..." she said sullenly. Hearing her say that she deserves it made me want to get up and go kick Jeremy's ass. How could someone tell another person that they deserved something like that?

"What type of abuse has he done?" I asked, lacing my fingers together and squeezing tightly.

"Physical, mental, verbal, and emotional abuse," she listed out softly. Softly enough that I almost couldn't hear her. I couldn't make an arrest though, we needed proof. If she reports it, I will make the arrest. That fucker will go down one way or another.

Remembering that she pushed and hit Jeremy brought up the question of, "If we leave... will you feel safe?" I saw her shake her head slowly and there was no way I was going to leave her alone. I would sit outside. I mentally hit my head. How was I supposed to look over her house if I didn't have a car? I sighed. "I'm going to have to leave for a bit. I can't watch your house to keep you safe without a car," I explained, and I saw the panic on her face.

"Please don't go," she whimpered, pulling her knees close to her. *How bad was this abuse?* It was going to be hard to be around Jeremy without the immediate reaction to want to do what I had done to Jaxon; kick the fucker's ass until there was nothing you could see of his face to identify him by. "You can sleep in the guest bedroom…" she offered, resting the side of her head onto her knees. "Wouldn't it be better to be inside keeping me safe?" And she was right, but this would be highly inappropriate, since I'm the detective on this case. Well, the Linda case. I couldn't do anything about the abuse, yet. I looked at her for a moment, seeing her pleading eyes.

Fuck me

"Stay here. I need to talk to Wilder." I then walked over to the door, placing my hand onto the handle. "You sure you want me to stay in your house?" I asked, looking over in her direction. I was giving her a chance to change her mind, but she nodded. I opened the door, walked out, and shut the door behind me. I looked down the hall and saw Wilder and Jeremy still talking. I took a few deep breaths to calm my anger, somewhat, and then headed down the hall towards them.

"Is she okay?" I heard Jeremy ask. I was avoiding looking at him, because if I did, then the anger would flare again. The last thing I needed was to beat the shit out of him while on duty; that wouldn't end well. *But if I was off duty…*

"She is fine," I said coldly, looking at Wilder. "I need to talk to you… in private." I noticed that Jeremy was going to walk by me, no doubt to go see Evelynn, but I stopped him as I placed my hand on his chest. "You can go home," I snapped, earning the look of confusion from both of them. "You can't go see her," I said, finally deciding to look at him. "She wants to be left alone," I said. *Especially from you,* I thought, removing my hand from his chest. "Go home," I warned him as I glared at him.

"The hell I can't!" Jeremy said and tried to head down the hall again, but I stepped in front of him. He was already irritating and pissed me off, and this persistence was not helping. By the look in his eyes, I knew he wanted to hit me, but I hope that he knew that it was his one-way ticket to jail. Wilder knew I was going to mentally snap, so he voiced in.

"Jeremy… it's in your best interest to just go home," he advised. Jeremy glared at me but then took a step back.

"Fine. I'll be back later to check on her… You can't keep me from doing that," he said as he turned to walk down the hall to the front door, but I needed to know one thing.

"Where were you last night when Linda was murdered?" I asked, stopping him in his tracks. He looked over his shoulder, not bothering to give us his full attention.

"I was working an overnight shift at the local grocery store and before you ask… I have an alibi." He then continued down the hall and went down the stairs. Soon after, we heard the front door shut.

Chapter Seven

Wilder

I don't know what was going on, but I was sure I was going to find out. I also knew I needed to tell Lockwood what I found out about Evelynn. This information, in my opinion, put her on the suspect list. As I heard the front door shut, I turned to Lockwood.

"So, what is it?" I asked and by the look on his face, I knew he was being hesitant. "Lockwood... just tell me," I pushed. He sighed and looked at me.

"I need to stay here tonight," he answered. Was I hearing him correctly? He didn't think that was a good idea, did he? It was my turn to sigh.

"You do realize how bad an idea that is right? Are you just going to sit outside without a car?" I asked but then came to the realization that that's not what he was going to do. "Lockwood... you can't be serious about staying in the house... you know that's not okay right? If the sergeant found out about this, he isn't going to like it..." I remarked, crossing my arms. What was he thinking?

"I'll be off the clock," he said defensively. "This has nothing to do with the Linda case," he explained, and I stayed silent, waiting for him to continue, and he got the hint. "Jeremy is abusing her... she told me herself. Now, she is scared to be alone because he will come back."

Remember how she pushed and hit him?" I nodded. "Well, he will take care of that when we leave," he finished, and I could hear the concern in his voice. Now was the time to tell him what I learned.

"I'm going to tell you what Jeremy told me, and I hope you will reconsider staying here…" I looked at him with a straight face, so he knew that this was serious. He gave me a confused look, so I continued, "We already know that she has mental health issues, considering the little outburst she had before going into her room." I was going to explain more to him, but he held up his hand to stop me.

"I could tell she has mental health issues… and I have concluded that it was severe, especially after what I witnessed when I went to her room… but I want her to tell me. I don't trust Jeremy in the slightest." He looked down the hall towards Evelynn's room and then back to me. "I told her we would eventually have to talk about it," he explained, "And since he is abusive with her and considering once we leave… he will come back to do god knows what… So, I'm staying," he said stubbornly. I could have argued with him about this, but I knew it wasn't worth it because if his mind was set on something, there was no changing it.

"How are you going to get off the clock if you're not leaving?" I asked, pretty much knowing what the answer would be.

"I'll call Samantha and tell her to clock me out." *Bingo*. I sighed and dragged my hand to the back of my head, not liking this at all.

"Okay. There is, as always, no way of changing your mind, so I'll drop it," I said, dropping my hand to my side. "Just be careful," I warned him. "Think about it… She has mental health issues, you don't know what it consists of, but there is a chance she could have something to do with Linda's death…" I said cautiously.

Lockwood sighed. "I know there is that chance, but it's a small one. I honestly don't think she is capable, but…" He looked down in the direction of Evelynn's room. "I'll keep my eyes on her."

I sighed, then looked down the hall for a moment, before heading down the stairs and out the door. This was irritating. He knows better than to do this, or so I thought. I walked towards the car, looking down the street at Linda's house.

This Sucks…

Chapter Eight

Evelynn

"So, I'm Staying," I heard Lockwood say.

I blew out the breath that I had been holding with relief, I had been eavesdropping to hear what was being said because I needed someone here. Usually, it was Linda, but that just wasn't possible anymore. I pushed and slapped Jeremy, which probably made him really pissed off at me. I didn't want to deal with the abuse; at least not today. So, my only option was to ask Detective Lockwood to stay. I couldn't ask Detective Wilder to stay as well because, based on the conversation they were having, he wouldn't have stayed. I didn't think he liked me very much either. I understood why they would be suspicious of me killing Linda, but I would never do that. There was no possible way that I could have. I was working on my deadline, and not once did I leave the house, I think if I would have killed Linda, I would know.

I couldn't believe Jeremy would reveal my mental health diagnosis to him, but I'm thankful that Lockwood said he didn't want to know yet; he wanted *me* to tell him. I'm almost positive that he will want to talk about it soon, but was I ready for it?

I moved away from the door and glanced at my Echo Show, it read 12:45 p.m. *Has it already been that long? Would he be able to clock out this early?* Knowing that Jeremy and Wilder left, I opened my bedroom door and stepped out. I looked down the hall and saw that Detective Lockwood was still there, on the phone. I headed down the hall and when I approached him, he hung up and turned to me.

"Feeling any better?" he asked, looking concerned, which made me quietly laugh.

"Yes," I replied, holding onto my genuine smile. I wanted to show him I was feeling better. The reason I wanted him to stay was because he felt safe. He made me feel safe, not because he was a cop, but as a person. He just witnessed one of my freak outs and just knew how to handle it. Yes, he probably has dealt with people like me, but it felt personal. I knew he needed the full truth about me. I just wasn't ready to tell him.

"What was that in there?" he asked calmly. *I had a feeling he was going to ask...* I needed to distract him from that topic. I looked around on the floor, not seeing my phone.

"Where is my phone?" I asked, looking at Lockwood.

Chapter Nine
Lockwood

She is trying to avoid talking about it... I sighed. I needed to know everything about her mental health for the investigation and my sanity. Wilder knew something that I needed to know, but I needed her to tell me, not by someone else. I wasn't going to betray her trust, like Jeremy had.

"Jeremy had it last..." I replied, looking at her to gauge her reaction. I heard her groan in frustration, as she dragged her hands down her face. "He has it... doesn't he?" I asked with the realization that Jeremy had taken it with him.

"Yeah, he does," she said with a sigh. "He does this sometimes... where he decides when he wants to take my phone from me," she explained as she headed downstairs. Another reason why I should have taken the phone from him. *I'm so dumb,* I thought as I followed her down the stairs.

"Where are you going?" I asked, already knowing the answer as she was putting her shoes on. She gave me the are-you-kidding-me look, as she finished.

"To go get my phone," she stated, as she opened the door to leave

"Wait!" I stopped her before she walked outside. She turned and gave me a confused look. "Wouldn't it be better if I just went to get your phone?" I asked, crossing my arms over my chest. "That way you wouldn't have to face him…"

"Oh no… you need me there," she said with a frustrated laugh. "If you go without me… he will be difficult… way more than if I was there. And we don't need you killing him," she said, giving me a look. "You think I didn't notice the look of murder on your face when I told you about the abuse?" She looked outside and then back at me. "So, are you coming?" I held my hands up in defeat.

"Okay… let's go…" I said with a sigh. We both headed out the door and she shut it behind us. "You're not going to lock the door?" I asked when I noticed her going down the path that led away from the house.

"No… we won't be gone that long," she said with no care. I then started to trail behind her.

"You do remember that there is a murderer out there, right?" I asked dumbfounded. "That was the reason why we came to talk to you." She turned to me and started walking backwards.

"Do all of you cops worry so much or is that just you?" she asked teasingly.

Just when it comes to you. I don't usually get this worked up towards anyone, but when it came to her, for some reason, I needed to be able to protect her.

"Anyways... It's daytime... I'm sure that a murderer isn't going to murder me or someone during the day..." she said matter-of-factly. "It's such a nice day..." she said looking up at the sky with a smile on her face. *You'd be surprised,* I thought, looking straight at her. It's nice to know that even though things were getting rough for her, she still was able to smile. "He only lives one street over... I'm sure walking would be a good idea!" She suggested as she turned right on the sidewalk and walked on. We walked in silence for a minute or two, but then she asked, "Why did you want to be a cop?"

I stayed silent for a moment then started to answer her question. "I was sixteen and living in Forestberg City," I said, looking ahead of me, as I recollected the memory. "It was two in the morning, and I was out roaming the city. I'll admit that I was not a good kid back then..." That statement earned me a small laugh from her. "What? It's one hundred percent true!" I exclaimed, with my own laugh.

"Okay, Mr. Bad Boy... What could you have possibly done that made you a bad kid?" she asked, nudging me with her shoulder and it sent a chill down my spine. That was the third time we touched each other, but when she moved slightly away, I wanted to feel more of her. I wanted to actually feel her skin. It just looked so soft.

"Well... I stole from different stores, started smoking and drinking when I was fifteen, started hard drugs at sixteen... didn't last long, I lost my virginity at 17..." I went silent and I had a sullen look on my face, but I quickly relaxed before she could see. I didn't want to open that can of worms yet, or if ever. "Anyways back to your question…" I said, changing the subject back to what we were originally talking about. "Like I said before… I was walking in the city and suddenly I heard a woman scream. I ran as fast as I could towards where the scream came from, and I saw that there was a male and female." The thought of what happened made my anger rise, but I needed to stay calm. "I saw that the woman was holding her stomach, and the male was holding a knife. As I got closer… I saw the blood. I ran and tackled the guy, beating him until he was unconscious. The woman… her name was Abby… had fallen to the ground and was in tears. She told me she was pregnant, so I took my phone out and called 9-1-1. Once the paramedics and cops came, I told them what I saw." I then sighed and ran my fingers through my hair. "Abby didn't make it… so both her and the baby died." I glanced over at Evelynn, seeing the sad look in her eyes. I stopped her from walking, turning her towards me and looked her straight in the eyes. "That's why I became a cop." Without thinking, I pulled her into my arms and surprisingly, she wrapped her arms around me.

Chapter Ten

Evelynn

Feeling his arms around me made me feel something I haven't felt in a long time, safe. Jeremy used to make me feel this way, but once the abuse started, that feeling didn't exist anymore. Even when he was holding me as I calmed down from my panic attacks, I felt on edge, but I let him hold me so I wouldn't make him mad. Once I calmed down though, I moved away because I didn't want him touching me more than what was needed. With Lockwood, I didn't want him to let go. I wanted to stay like this for as long as possible, but I needed my phone back.

"Come on… let's go get my phone back," I said as I reluctantly let go of him. He held onto me for a second longer before letting me go. We continued walking, soon coming to Jeremy's street. "His house is halfway down," I said, as I started walking down the street.

"Me being with you is going to shock the hell out of him," Lockwood said with a smirk of amusement. "Since I shouldn't even be here right now. I mean he probably thought I would be gone by now," he quickly clarified.

"His face is going to be priceless," I said with a small laugh. "But… you're here to protect me. He won't do anything while you're with me," I said, smiling up at him and he looked down at me returning the smile. He had such a gorgeous smile. These are one of the moments when I wished I had my phone on me.

"So…" I began, looking down at the ground. "Am I supposed to keep referring to you as Detective Lockwood or can I call you Bradley?" I asked with a hint of teasing. At this point it just felt weird calling him something formally. I looked ahead of us, seeing that we were nearing Jeremy's house.

"You can call me Bradley," he chuckled as he nudged me with his shoulder, though it was more his arm than shoulder. Our hands touched with that movement, which made me stop walking and look down at our hands. I wanted so much to hold his hand, but all that happened was our fingers brushing up against each other a few times. We looked at each other for a moment or two, before we both looked away.

We started walking again and soon came to Jeremy's house, but I stopped short and just looked at it. *I don't want to be here;* I thought as my anxiety slightly rose. I may have talked all high and mighty about coming here, but I was terrified of being here. I told myself I wouldn't ever come back here because he nearly killed me inside that house. He beat the shit out of me, and it landed me into the hospital. I couldn't tell anyone the truth because everyone believed his story. I was unconscious when the lie came out of his mouth.

"Evelynn… you okay?" I snapped out of whatever trance I was in when I heard Bradley speak and I looked at him.

"Yeah... I'm fine," I lied, starting to walk towards the front door. I didn't get very far because I felt Bradley's hand grab onto my arm, pulling me back.

"You're not fine," he said bluntly. He looked at me with his eyebrows raised. "I'm a cop, remember... I can tell when a person is lying... and I am good at my job." He added the last bit to make me nervous so I wouldn't continue with my lie.

"No, I'm not fine," I said, sighing and looking at the ground. I suddenly felt a finger underneath my chin, guiding me to look up at Bradley. "Not here..." I quickly said, knowing what he was going to ask. "I'll tell you later," I promised. He was learning a lot about my life, my current life today. But there was a lot about me and my life that he didn't know, and I had a feeling he would learn most of it soon.

He studied my face, until he was content with my answer and removed his finger from me. I then realized that I was breathing slightly heavily. Not because of anxiety, but because he was so close to me. All I could think about was wanting him to kiss me. I wanted to feel his lips against mine. Looking at him made me forget all about my anxiety. That was short lived when he started walking to the front door. I followed close behind, until we were standing right in front of it.

I took a deep breath in and slowly let it out, as I knocked on the door. Usually, I was able to just walk in, if it was unlocked, but didn't this time because Bradley was here too. I rarely came here anyway, so I didn't think it would matter if I knocked or not. I heard footsteps coming towards the door and when it opened, it revealed Jeremy. He looked between me and Bradley with confusion.

"Well, I'm surprised that you're here," Jeremy said pointing at me. He then moved his hand to point at Bradley, "But I'm *really* surprised that you're here... Shouldn't you be working?" he asked as he dropped his hand.

"Off the clock," was all Bradley said and by the looks of it, he was trying to hold himself back. I knew he wanted nothing more than to beat the shit out of Jeremy, but this was not the time.

"Where's my phone Jeremy?" I asked with annoyance. He was clearly not listening to me, because he was still looking at Bradley.

"If you're off the clock... then why aren't you at home... or at the bar? Don't you guys do that after a long shift?" Jeremy asked cockily. This was not going to end well if Jeremy kept this attitude up. I could feel the tension radiating from Bradley next to me.

"Jeremy! Phone!" I snapped, holding my hand out to him. He closed his eyes and laughed his low, dangerous laugh, which made a shudder go down my spine. His attention was on me now, but I kept reminding myself that he couldn't do anything.

"I don't have your phone, Evie," he said, exasperated, folding his arms in front of him and leaning against the doorframe. "I put it on the back of the couch before I left." Was he kidding me? I let out a frustrated sigh, holding the bridge of my nose with my pointer finger and thumb.

"I don't have time for this, Jeremy!" I said, trying to keep it together. It would be wise for me to try not to act like I had before. "It was not on the couch. I would have seen it." I looked at him and he shrugged his shoulders.

"I don't know what to tell you, Eve." He pushed off the doorframe. "Now excuse me, but I'm in no mood to socialize… Since, you know… I was kicked out of my best friend's house and now I see I can't spend time with her now…" He was glaring at Bradley, while speaking. "Call me when he is gone." He then shut the door, leaving us just staring at it.

"I can't believe him," I said, kicking Jeremy's door out of frustration. I turned to Bradley. "If you were on the clock…, would you be able to do something?" I asked him. He was silent for a moment, as he was thinking and rubbing his chin.

"In a sense, yes, but we would need to see if your phone is indeed there," he said cautiously. I groaned loudly, stomping down the stairs and down the path from Jeremy's house to the sidewalk. I was definitely playing with fire, raging fire. Why am I doing this to myself? Was it because Bradley is with me? *Fuck! Bradley is only staying one night and then I'm defenseless.* With what is coming, it would actually be my fault.

48

"I need to get away from here… I can't be here…" I told Bradley as he approached me.

Chapter Eleven

Lockwood

I was nervous for her. I knew how scared of him she was, but she was standing up to him? How was I supposed to leave tomorrow? After what just happened here, it was not going to end well for her. I wanted to just stay with her for as long as possible, to protect her, but I needed to find out who murdered Linda. Me staying there with her would probably be worse for her though.

I walked away from the house and went to where Evelynn was. As I approached her, I heard her say that she needed to get away from here; that she can't be here. Something bad happened here and I would soon find out, since she said she would tell me. We started walking, but in silence. I figured she was sorting through her thoughts, and I would give her that moment.

We soon made it to her house, and I noticed that she was looking at Linda's house, but then she quickly went inside. When I followed in after her, I saw her frozen on the spot. I looked to where she was looking, seeing that her phone was in fact there on the couch. I was just as shocked as her.

"I must have overlooked it," she mumbled, obviously upset. She turned and walked past me, heading towards the kitchen

I ran a hand through my hair, staring at her phone. *I could have prevented this,* I thought as I dropped my hand to my side. There was something far worse that was going on between Evelynn and Jeremy and I was going to find out what it was. I looked at her phone one more time, before I headed after her. Upon entering the kitchen, I saw Evelynn take a shot of something. I looked to the right of her and saw that there was this clear liquid in a green, transparent alien head.

"It's called Outer Space Vodka," I heard her say. I watched her pour the vodka into two shot glasses. She beckoned me over by tapping the counter. I walked over to her, and she slid the second shot over to me. "We are getting wasted." She smiled and I could see traces of excitement, which made me smile back at her.

"It's only two," I said with a short laugh. "Not to mention… I work tomorrow." I hated saying those words, especially when I saw her face fall. "Anyways… If I'm staying the night, I'm gonna need slumber party essentials," I teased, taking the shot glass from her and placing it on the counter. When I looked at her, I saw terror in her eyes. "Relax," I said, placing my hands on the sides of her face and looking right in her eyes. "You're coming with me," I said softly. I wanted so much to kiss her at that moment, our faces were so close to each other, but that would be crossing a line. Our actions were already so close to crossing that I needed to dial things back. Honestly, it was bad enough that I agreed to sleep here, but the need to protect her was great.

I moved away from her and looked at the alien head. "Based on how you have decorated your house... I am shocked to see you with this," I said, tipping the head back to get a better look at its face. I could just feel the disappointment and hurt radiating off her and it was internally tormenting me. I placed the alien head back on the counter and looked at her. "Come on... let's go get my stuff." I then chuckled. "You are my ride." I wanted to lighten the mood just to see that sweet smile of hers again. A soft laugh was returned as she looked up at me.

"Yeah, I guess that is true," she said with amusement. "Why don't you drive since you probably know how to get there," she suggested. I was hesitant to answer, but then I finally spoke up.

"Yeah, we can do that," I said, with a smile. It was hard not to smile at her when she was smiling at me, even after I had offended her. "It seems logical enough... Well, let's get going then!" I perked up. "Where are your keys?"

"In my bag," she answered as she turned and headed out of the kitchen. I couldn't help but glance at her butt and oh my god, it was perfect. It was just so round, perky, and had the right amount of bounce to it. It gave me the come-hither vibes, and I wanted to give into the temptation. I felt myself growing hard and it snapped me out of my thoughts, at the same time as Evelynn asked me a question, which I didn't pick up.

"What?" I asked like a damn idiot. I heard her giggle, and my face probably became red from when I realized that I was hard. *Just what I needed. Face red and a damn erection,* I thought as I looked down at my feet to hide my embarrassment.

"I asked if you were coming…" she repeated with a smirk. I really hoped she didn't see the bulge that probably was showing through my jeans.

Should have stayed with my first idea of wearing my black slacks, I thought with an internal sigh. "Yeah, I'm coming." It kind of sounded like I stumbled through the words, but I needed to compose myself. *Nothing can happen between us,* and as I thought those words, I barely believed them.

"You okay?" she asked, concern written all over her face.

"Yeah, I'm fine… Let's go," I replied with irritation and started walking towards her, slid past her, and headed down the hall.

Chapter Twelve

Jeremy

I looked through the curtains, watching them until they left. I finished off my whisky that I was drinking before they showed up. *What the hell was **he** still doing around? And he was off the clock? Isn't there some rule about cops being around the people involved in an investigating case?* I could easily call and report him, but I would think detective Wilder would say something, wouldn't he?

I was gripping my glass so tight that I didn't even notice, until the glass shattered into pieces. I looked down at my bloody hand, watching the blood drip down onto the glass pieces. I let out a low growl. *That was my favorite glass,* I thought as I went to go and take care of my hand.

When I found my first aid kit in the bathroom, I set everything down on the counter and got to work on my hand. There were a few deep cuts, but I wasn't worried about them; I didn't think they needed stitches anyways. When I finished tending to my hand, I was still fuming at the sight of Lockwood being there with her. When I heard them talking from outside, I happened to see their little sentimental moment, before they came up to my door. I almost went out there to kick that detective's ass, but they didn't need to know that I knew about it. They were getting too friendly, and I didn't like it one bit. Evelynn should know better than to piss me off, and that's exactly what was happening.

Chapter Thirteen

Evelynn

We had been driving for ten minutes now, and we hadn't spoken a word to each other. Why was he so upset? What happened between us talking and then leaving the kitchen? I hope I didn't do anything, but I couldn't see how I would have. I kept replaying that moment repeatedly, but I couldn't pinpoint what could have happened. I wish he would just talk to me; tell me why he was upset. I glanced at him a few times and noticed him wincing when we made turns.

"Are you okay?" I asked, finally breaking the silence. "You keep wincing every time you make a turn," I pointed out. He looked at me for a second from the corner of his eye, then back on the road.

"I was shot in my right shoulder, and it didn't heal properly. So, some things I do hurt. Sometimes it can get pretty bad, but I manage," he explained as he drove into an apartment complex. I looked around the area and it wasn't what I expected. I was expecting a lavish house or an expensive apartment, but it was just an ordinary apartment building. I looked back at him as he parked in a parking spot. I watched as he massaged his right shoulder.

"You should have told me about your shoulder." I sighed. "I wouldn't have had you drive," I stated, feeling bad about it. He shrugged like it was no big deal and opened the car door.

"Come on." He smiled, using his head to point towards his building. We both got out of the car and started to walk through the parking lot, until we came to the building door. He took out his keys and jumbled through them, until he found the right one. He had a lot of keys, and it piqued my curiosity.

"Why so many keys?" I asked with confusion on my face. He smiled as he unlocked the door.

"For different things," he said vaguely, pulling the door open. "Ladies first." He swooped his arm towards the entrance.

"Why, thank you," I said with a little curtsy and then walked into the building. He walked in behind me and headed over to the stairs. He then turned to me as I came to his side.

"I'm on the second floor, so we don't need to climb too many stairs," he said as he started up the stairs. I followed behind until we came to his floor. He took a left and walked about halfway down the hall, until we were in front of his apartment door. He unlocked the door, but before he opened it, he turned to me. "Just to warn you... my place is a mess," he said. "I don't usually have guests and with my job it gets challenging to pick up around the apartment," he explained. I could tell he was embarrassed, and it caused me to smile.

"No worries... I'm not bothered about the state of your home," I reassured him. He nodded and took a deep breath in and then slowly let it out. He opened the door and stepped inside, letting me come into the front area of the apartment.

I looked around, seeing that in front of us was the living room and I could see what he meant about it being a mess. There were clothes everywhere, all different sorts of trash littered around the room, among other random things. The apartment wasn't big so maybe it looked worse than it was.

I looked at Bradley, who was scratching the back of his head awkwardly. "Yeah, this is home sweet home," he said jokingly. "Would you be okay with me jumping in the shower quickly?" he asked, dropping his arm to his side.

"Knock yourself out," I said with a smile. I was trying not to picture him in the shower, but that failed epically. I moved into the living room area and saw that there was a dark brown leather couch that was mostly covered in clothes and a blanket. I noticed a pillow too. Did he sleep there? It made me worried about what his bedroom looked like.

"Okay, well... There is water and pop in the fridge. There is some food, but not a whole lot since I usually do take out," he offered. I didn't want him to feel awkward or anything, so I shooed him.

"Go take your shower..." I ordered as I pushed him towards the hallway. It wasn't a long hallway, so I was able to see where the bathroom was.

"I'm going, I'm going," he laughed as he walked down the hallway more. "See you in a few." He then went into what I assumed was his bedroom, and then a few moments later he had gone into the bathroom. Once I heard the water running, I went into the kitchen, which was behind the wall where the couch was and started looking for the garbage bags. He was doing so much for me, so why not help him clean up a little? It wasn't much compared to what he had been doing for me, but it was something, right? Once I located the garbage bags, I started to get to work.

Chapter Fourteen

Lockwood

As I stood in the shower, letting the water fall onto the entirety of my body, I couldn't keep her out of my mind, and she was only in the living room! I needed to start figuring out what happened to Linda. *You're letting a girl affect your life again,* I thought, with a sigh. Last time I was interested in a girl I invested all my time with her. This was different, though. Evelynn was perfect and I decided to stay with her overnight at her house because of her abusive friend. Once I leave tomorrow, who knows what will happen. I had a job to do, though. She would understand that since it was her friend that was murdered, right?

What bothered me the most about Evelynn was that I haven't kissed her, even though I so much wanted to. There were so many opportunities to do so, but I just didn't do anything. I know she wanted me to kiss her, but I just couldn't do it. I was on the investigation that involved her, and that would cross so many lines. I wanted to so fucking bad though.

I moved away from under the water and quickly finished up in the shower, not wanting her to wait much longer. As I went to start getting dressed, I noticed that I had forgotten boxers. The issue with that though was that my clean boxers were still in the living room, since I haven't had the chance to put the clothes away.

"Fuck..." I whispered, putting my hand on the door handle. I had a towel wrapped around my waist, so it wasn't like she was going to see anything, but it still felt embarrassing.

I sighed and opened the door, heading down the short hallway, holding the towel in place and walking into the living room. When I came into the living space, I didn't expect to see Evelynn cleaning. It looked like she was picking up the garbage that had been scattered around the area since she had a garbage bag in her hands. I wasn't sure if I should announce my presence or just quietly get what I needed and sneak back into the bathroom. I was going to go with the latter, but my towel fell, just as she turned around. I froze as we just stared at each other in shock. The wheels were turning in her mind, as she looked me up and down, stopping for a brief moment on my member and then back at me. Which, in turn, made me even more embarrassed.

"I... I was just um... I forgot boxers," I said awkwardly, grabbing the first boxers I saw that were in the clean pile, and quickly putting them on. "I'll just... go finish getting dressed," I said as I quickly turned and headed back to the bathroom.

When I was back in the bathroom, I internally kicked myself. I couldn't believe that my towel had fallen and that she saw *everything*! What embarrassed me most was that she saw my dick, and she lingered on it for a moment. What did she think? I shook my head; it doesn't matter right now. There were more important things to worry about. I had to keep her safe no matter what. I just didn't know how I was going to do that when I left tomorrow. I sighed as I started to get dressed. *What am I supposed to do?* I thought as I finished getting dressed and looked into the mirror, just thinking what the next steps were. I pushed off the sink, not wanting to keep her waiting.

Chapter Fifteen
Evelynn

Once I heard the bathroom door close, I snapped out of whatever trance I was in. "Wow..." I whispered, in awe of his body. Then there was his member. I let out a quick breath and shook my head. *Focus,* I thought as I looked around the room. It looked better but needed some more work. I looked over at the pile of clothes that were on the couch, assuming those were clean since he grabbed boxers from there.

Maybe I should stop... I pondered, but to my right there was an empty clothes basket. *Just the clothes on the floor,* I thought as I started picking up the dirty clothes around the living room and placed them in the basket.

"You didn't have to do this," I heard Bradley say suddenly, which caused me to jump and turn to him, placing my right hand over my heart.

"Jesus... you didn't have to scare me!" I exclaimed, letting out a long breath. I looked around the room. "Well, there really isn't much to do, so I thought I would help out a little bit," I said with a shrug, "and it's a thank you for staying with me... I know it's probably something you are not supposed to do, but I appreciate it." I smiled, then a thought crossed my mind. I don't think he would agree to it, but it was worth a shot. "Ummm... do you think I could stay here with you instead?" I asked nervously. "I don't want to burden you... I just thought staying here would keep me safer... since Jeremy doesn't know where you live." I couldn't look at him. I was just so nervous about what he would say. It didn't help my nerves as he stayed silent. I didn't know what he was thinking. *Why would I just invite myself to stay? He must think I'm stupid for asking,* I thought, internally kicking myself.

"Yeah... I think that would be a better idea, since I really do have to go to work tomorrow," he said in agreement, which was a relief. He then let out a small laugh. "Probably means we have to go back to get things for you."

"If you're okay with that?" I asked, a little worried about being too much of a burden. "I realized that I left my phone at home, and I need my laptop for 'work'," I said with air quotes. I didn't think what I did for a living was work, but others have said that it technically is, but I thought of it as more of a self-care thing.

"What do you do for work?" he asked curiously. I bet he was wondering about that the moment he saw my house. For some reason everyone is shocked by the fact that I have a nice house, since they didn't think I was earning enough to have a beautiful home. With hard work, budgeting, and saving money though, I was able to afford it.

"It might surprise you... It seems to do that to everyone else, but I do have fans that love my work," I said, but then I noticed the confusion on his face, which made me smile a little. After a moment I said, "I'm an author." And there it was, the look of surprise.

"That *is* surprising, but I think that it's great!" he exclaimed. "I wonder why I have never seen your name on any books…" he pondered, scratching the back of his head.

"That's because I use a pen name," I explained. "For safety reasons… not like I'm in immediate danger, but it's a just in case thing." Ever since the night my dad died, I didn't want to risk being found by the people who murdered him. The night he died, it almost seemed personal, and I felt threatened by the murderers.

"What is your pen name?" he asked with curiosity.

"Let's just go get my stuff and we can talk more about it later," I said, heading towards the door. I liked leaving things as a mystery when it came to my author career.

"This is going to bother me until you tell me," He teased, as he followed me.

"Well… you just have to wait." I winked at him, and we then went out the door.

***

We got to the door of my house, but the door looked like it was ajar. I looked at Bradley with worry. Who was or had been in my house? I was about to walk in, but Bradley stopped me. I looked at him and noticed he had his gun in his hand. I stepped to the side, as he cautiously pushed open the door.

Chapter Sixteen

Lockwood

I didn't know what I was going to find, but for her protection, I had to search the house. I may not be on the clock, but sometimes, I still need to get into that role to keep others safe. Though, with the Jaxon incident, my anger got the best of me, and I was being stupid. I was never able to control my anger, but with having to do anger management classes and working with the therapist that was provided through work, I was able to control it better.

"Stay here…" I slowly walked into the house and since it was evening, it was dark inside. I felt around the wall that was on the right side of the door, soon finding the light switch. When I switched it on, the entryway had things scattered around on the floor. I saw a switch on a wall in front of me, so I quickly walked over to it and flipped it on. It lit up the living room and I didn't like what I saw. The living room was completely trashed, but what didn't sit well with me was that the word MURDERER was written on one of the walls, it seemed like it was written in blood, and I noticed that it was splattered on the floor as well. I didn't know if I wanted to know whose blood it belonged to, but with my line of work, I needed to know. It just made me worry about Evelynn finding out whose blood it was.

I backed away from the living room and into the view of her. "I'm going to search the rest of the house... Just stay out there," I instructed. I then started searching the house. In every room, I saw that everything was thrown or shattered on the floors, beds, and counters. There was only one person I could think of that would do this... Jeremy. Why would he write murderer on her wall? I now definitely had questions for Evelynn, but luckily there was no one in the house. *I'm gonna have to get Wilder here,* I thought as I took out my phone. I brought up Wilder's number and listened to it ring, until he answered.

"Wilder... I have a situation, and I need the whole team to come," I said, when he finally answered after the fourth ring.

"What's going on?" he asked leerily, and I didn't blame him. I didn't straight out tell him what happened.

"Evelynn and I left her house to pick up things from my house and when we got back, her place had been broken into and they trashed it," I explained, as I headed towards the stairs and climbed down them.

"So... Why do we need the whole team?" he questioned and rightly so.

"Here is the kicker..." I began, a little worried that he might pin Linda's death on Evelynn. I had to tell him though; he was going to see it anyway. "One of the walls in the living room had '*murderer*' written on it, with blood." I looked towards the open front door, but Evelynn wasn't there. I looked towards the living room and saw her standing in the middle of the room, staring at the accusatory word. When I looked closer at her, I noticed that her shoulders were moving up and down, in a way that indicated that she was having a panic attack. *Shit.*

"I gotta go," I said quickly and hung up, without giving Wilder a chance to answer. I raced into the kitchen and started searching for her anxiety meds, but they weren't there. I then remembered that Jeremy had given her the last one in the kitchen. I ran back upstairs and went into the bathroom, figuring they would be in there, since that was where she was going this morning to get one. I searched and searched, but they weren't in there either. *Where the fuck could they be?* I stood there trying to think where else they could be. *Her bag!* I ran back down the stairs, remembering that her bag was by the front door, since she didn't take it with her when we left. Once I made it, I started digging through it; worrying that they weren't there either and of course they weren't. "Fuck!" I yelled, standing up from the crouch position.

I looked back at where Evelynn was and saw that she was curled up on the floor. I could now hear her breathing loud and clear, then it dawned on me what else she was doing. I ran to her and saw that she was scratching her arm. It was much worse than before. This time she was scratching so hard that it was making her bleed. I dropped down next to her, pulling her in my arms, and moved her hand away from her arm.

"Evelynn… I know it will be hard… but I need you to breathe with me…" I told her, as I rocked her. "I couldn't find any of your meds… so I need you to work with me…"

I pleaded. This had to work, or she could pass out. I placed her hand on my chest and started to take deep breaths, so she could try matching her breathing with mine. Why couldn't I find her meds? I looked everywhere that I thought they would be. It then dawned on me. Jeremy must have taken them. *He isn't going to get away with that,* I thought as I continued my deep breaths.

"It's going to be okay, baby…" I said subconsciously. "Just slow your breathing… It's going to be fine." At this point I didn't know if I was trying to convince myself as well. Her breathing was slowly getting better; she wasn't audible anymore, but she was still breathing heavily. "You're doing good, sweetheart… just keep doing what you're doing… keep breathing with me…"

I soon heard sirens and saw the blue and red flashing of the cruiser's lights. I wouldn't move even if they wanted me to. I wasn't leaving her. Soon, there was a knock on the door. She grabbed my shirt, not wanting me to leave her alone.

"Get in here!" I called out to them, not knowing if they could hear me or not. I turned my attention back to Evelynn. "It's okay… I'm staying here…" I reassured her. Her breathing was becoming slower and more controlled. "You're doing so well…"

I heard the front door open, and I heard the voices of my team, but they seemed so distant, since I was too invested in getting Evelynn to continue to slow her breathing. I didn't know Wilder came over to us, until he placed a hand on my shoulder.

"Let me take over…" he said in a soft voice. "You know I'm good with this…" It was true that he was good

with this, but she wanted me with her. He tried moving me away, but I jerked my arm away.

"She wants me!" I exclaimed, tightening my hold on her. "Her breathing is getting back to normal," I said, feeling that she was taking deep breaths and matching my breathing. "Keep taking those deep breaths… it's going to be over soon," I said softly into her ear. After a moment or two, her breathing was finally back to normal. "Good job… you did great…"

Chapter Seventeen

Wilder

When the investigation team and I made it to Evelynn's house, we all hurried out of our vehicles. We had a quick discussion, before heading towards the house. I made a quick glance at Linda's house before knocking on Evelynn's door. A moment passed and I was about to knock again, but I then heard Lockwood call us in. It seemed odd that they didn't come to the door, but I opened it.

"Stay here until I call you in," I told the team. Then, I walked in, shutting the door behind me. I didn't see Lockwood or Evelynn, but I did hear Lockwood's voice. I walked over to where the living room was and saw them both on the floor; Lockwood was holding onto Evelynn. I looked around the room, seeing how everything had been thrown everywhere and then I saw it. The word murderer on the wall that Lockwood had mentioned. At first, I thought it was Evelynn's blood, but when I looked back at them, I could see that Evelynn was unhurt but breathing heavily. *Panic attack,* I thought as I walked over to them. I placed my hand on Lockwood's shoulder.

"Let me take over…" I told Lockwood softly, not wanting to alarm them. "You know I'm good with this…" I reminded him, as I tried pulling him away from her, but he just pulled his arm away.

"She wants me!" he exclaimed. "Her breathing is getting back to normal…" he said calmly.

At that point I just backed away, until she calmed down enough to separate them. I needed to talk to Lockwood alone. After a few minutes, her breathing went back to normal, but he wouldn't move from her. He just continued to hold her.

"I need to bring the investigation team in to start figuring out what exactly happened here," I said, then looked at the bloody word. "And to see whose blood that belongs to," I mumbled. When I saw the nod of approval from him, I went and got the team. Everyone poured in, with their equipment, and got to work. I went back to Lockwood and Evelynn.

"Lockwood…" I said sternly. "We need to talk…" I wasn't going to take no for an answer; verbally or nonverbally. When he didn't show any inkling of moving, Evelynn spoke up.

"I'm okay now, Bradley…" she reassured him. "Go talk to him. You are part of this investigation too," she added as she moved away from him and that's when I noticed her arm. It was scratched up badly to the point of bleeding. I turned to one of the police officers that joined. Why we needed the extra cops is beyond me, but the sergeant sent them, so I couldn't really tell them we didn't need them.

"Go back to one of the cars and get a first aid kit." I turned and looked at her arm again. "Clean her arm and bandage it up," I instructed.

"Yes sir," The officer replied, then disappeared out the front door. I turned back to Lockwood. "You... with me." I pointed at him and crooked my finger a few times, to indicate to follow me. He sighed and reluctantly stood up, telling Evelynn he would be back and then followed me to the kitchen, which was also a huge mess. "You seem to care about her... *too* much," I said, turning to him and crossing my arms over my chest. "Is this going to be like —" before I could finish, Lockwood interrupted me.

"Don't bring her into this..." he warned me. He never wanted to talk about what happened with his ex-wife.

"Fine, but don't let Evelynn distract you from what needs to be done," I said sternly. "So... Evelynn's house looks like a tornado came through it and the word murderer is painted on her wall with what appears to be blood..." I started to say, but then I saw him about to say something, so I put my hand up to stop him. "Let me finish... the word murderer is on her living room wall, Lockwood... doesn't that raise any red flags?" I hissed, as I stepped closer to him.

"I know *exactly* who did this!" he hissed back, also taking a step towards me.

"And who exactly do you think wrote that and destroyed her house?" I asked a little louder. *This should be good.* Suddenly we started to hear yelling from the front door.

"Evelynn!" We heard Jeremy call out and the look of murder appeared on Lockwood's face.

Chapter Eighteen
Lockwood

"Lockwood! Don't!" I barely heard Wilder over the sound of my blood pumping in my ears, as I quickly stormed out of the kitchen and bee lined towards Jeremy. Once I was close enough, I punched him as hard as I could and pushed him against the wall, placing my forearm into his throat.

"You're a fucking prick!" I yelled into his face. "You will pay for everything you have done to her!" At that moment I was being pulled away from him by two of the cops that were there.

"What the fuck are you talking about?" Jeremy asked loudly, rubbing his neck.

"Look the fuck around you!" I growled, as I tried to get to him again, but the two cops pulled me back.

"I didn't do this!" Jeremy yelled.

"Fuck you! You would do anything to ruin her life!" If he said two more words, I would probably start seeing red. Before anything more could happen, there was a shattering sound and the sound of Evelynn screaming. I snapped my head in her direction and saw her crouch down, covering her head with her arms. Glass flew as far as it could go, covering the floor and her.

"Let go of me!" I yelled as I pulled away from the cops, racing to Evelynn's side. I helped her up and brushed off all the glass that was on her.

"So… we just met Lockwood this morning and now he thinks he can just stake claim on Evelynn?" Jeremy asked angrily.

"Shut up, Jeremy!" Evelynn snapped. "No one can claim me. I shouldn't be someone who has to be owned…" she said annoyed. All I did was glare at him, holding restraint on myself from going after him again.

Wilder walked over to what was thrown through the window, seeing that it was a brick and there was writing on it.

She Will Die

"McMillan! Anderson! Get out there and find who threw this!" Wilder barked at the two cops that had been holding me back from beating the shit out of Jeremy. I watched as they ran out of the house. Wilder then turned to the forensic investigators. "Get fingerprints off the brick!" he demanded, as he walked over to us. "You okay, Evelynn?" he asked, which threw me off because he just accused Evelynn of murder.

"Yeah… I'm fine," she responded with a small smile. She then turned to me. "I don't want to be here anymore," she said, and I could see how scared she was, and I don't blame her for feeling that way.

"Is there someone you can stay with?" Wilder asked her.

"She can stay with me," Jeremy piped in, acting like he actually cared about her safety when she was in danger with him.

"The fuck she will!" I snapped looking at Jeremy. "She will be staying with me," I stated, looking at Wilder. He didn't seem too fond of the idea, but he knew not to argue with me, since the plan was already decided that I was going to stay here for the night. It really didn't matter where she stayed, as long as it was with me. So, all he did was nod.

"Then hurry and get her out of here," he said, just as the two cops came back into the house.

"Sir... there was no one around that we could see," McMillan said. "And no indication that someone was there."

"Well, it did look like there could have been footprints, but they have been kicked away or covered up with dirt." Anderson added on.

"And there are no fingerprints on the brick or anywhere in the house," One of the forensic investigators said. "Which means whoever did this was most likely wearing gloves."

Wilder turned to us. "Why are you still here?" he asked with irritation. "Get out of here!" he demanded.

I nodded and looked at Evelynn. "Get what you can and then we can leave," I said as calmly as I could. I was still riled up from my altercation with Jeremy, who, for some reason, was still here.

"This is *so* not right!" Jeremy exclaimed. "Her staying with *him*..." he started, and he was two seconds away from me going after him again. "It's so unprofessional... maybe I should call—"

"Get him out of here!" Wilder demanded. "He is obstructing the investigation..." he said, which caused me to smirk. Evelynn, at this point, went off to get what she needed. Anderson took Jeremy's arm to lead him out, but he whipped his arm away.

"That is no reason for me having to leave!" he yelled, as the cop tried ushering him out of the house, but he was still fighting.

"Do *not* make me arrest you!" Wilder snapped.

"For what!?" Jeremy yelled at Wilder.

"For not being compliant with law enforcement... Now leave!" Wilder was not one to take anyone's shit. Evelynn soon came back with a bag, but I did notice that her eyes were red and puffy.

"What's wrong?" I asked her with concern. Jeremy finally walked out of the house, but it didn't mean he wouldn't be outside waiting.

"Can we just go?" Evelynn asked, as she wiped her eyes with one of her hands.

"Yeah... let's go," I said, wrapping an arm around her shoulders and leading her out of the house. Once we were out of the house, my suspicion was correct. Jeremy was outside waiting for us.

"You will both regret everything..." Was all he said, before walking away from the house and down the street. I then led Evelynn to her car and put her in the passenger seat. I took her bag from her and tossed it in the backseat. I went and got into the driver's seat, taking her car keys out of my pocket and starting up the car. I looked at her for a moment, then pulled out of the driveway and started driving.

Chapter Nineteen

Evelynn

Throughout most of the drive, I stayed silent. I kept wondering who was doing this to me. I didn't see what was written on the brick because I wanted out of my own house. The house I worked so hard to get and that I loved, but now... I couldn't feel safe there.

"Whoever did this... broke my laptop..." I said softly, but loud enough for Bradley to hear me. "It was broken in half... luckily I have my work on a flash drive and it's in my day-to-day bag..." I said, holding my bag up. "But... I had pictures on there that I hadn't backed up yet and they were so important to me... I feel so dumb not backing them up right away..."

"Are they on your phone?" he asked me, glancing in my direction, before putting his eyes back on the road.

"That was broken too, since I had left it there and the SD card was snapped in half... they are just... gone," I whimpered in the last part. I didn't want to cry again, but tears fell down my face. I suddenly felt his fingers intertwining with mine and just holding my hand.

"Everything will be fine... we will find who did this to you," he said, glancing over at me for a moment. "I promise," he said reassuringly, as his eyes went back onto the road. I assumed that he thought it was Jeremy who did this, and I couldn't help but agree with him.

***

When we got back to his apartment and were inside, I collapsed onto his couch, next to the clean pile of clothes. I looked at the pile and grabbed a shirt, starting to fold it. Then I did it with the next article of clothing.

"You don't need to do that..." Bradley spoke up. "You can go lay in my bed and just rest... You must be exhausted after everything," he said with concern.

"Will you lay with me? At least until I fall asleep?" I asked, not wanting to be left alone. He picked up on that and held out his hand to me.

"Come on," he said as he helped me stand up. He led me down the hall and into his room. There really wasn't much in his room, but it was still welcoming, especially his bed. There was a queen-sized bed, a flat screen TV that was mounted on the wall right across from it, nothing else on the white walls, but there was a short dresser with pictures on it.

I walked over to the pictures and looked at them, feeling Bradley's eyes on me. There was one picture that caught my attention. It was a picture of him and a little girl. The small child looked like him. She had beautiful long wavy brown hair, and pretty, green eyes. She couldn't be older than five years old.

"Who is this?" I asked, turning to him. I could see the pain and sadness in his eyes.

"My daughter…" he mumbled, as he walked over to me, taking the picture from me. He looked at it for a moment and I could just see he was hurting emotionally.

"What happened to her?" I asked softly. I could tell that this was a hard topic, so if he didn't want to talk about it, then I would leave it alone.

"Information for information?" he asked, looking me in the eyes. When he saw me nod in agreement, he continued, "I got married three years ago, but we ended up getting a divorce… a year later… We just weren't getting along, and she didn't like me being a cop, because I was barely around… So, to try and fix the marriage, I worked shorter hours to spend more time with them, but it wasn't enough… So, she left and took our daughter with her… I haven't seen her since… She would be nine years old now," he said sullenly, as he placed the picture back in its proper place.

"Did you try looking for them?" I asked with curiosity.

"I did and I found them a year later, but when I approached the house, they were living in, I saw my daughter in the living room…" He went silent for a moment, "There was a guy with her, and they looked so happy, it looked like they were playing a game of some sort. Then joy grew on her face when she saw her mom. I haven't seen my little girl smile like that in so long." He paused as he wiped tears from his eyes. "I didn't want to ruin that by causing chaos with my presence. So, I went back to my car and reluctantly left," he finished, but he let out a small laugh. "I almost barged in there, because I will admit that anger took over, but what good would that have done…"

"I am so sorry…" I said softly. I didn't know what to say beyond that. I don't think anything would make it better for him. Not being able to see your own child must be so hard. Instead of saying anything more, I just wrapped my arms around his waist. I wanted to comfort him, and this was the only thing I could do. I felt his arms around me, as he laid his head on mine. We stayed like this for a little bit, before I looked up at him and he looked back down at me. I didn't expect it, but he slowly leaned down, hovering over my mouth.

"I'm so happy I found you, though," he whispered and then our mouths connected. It felt like an electric current went through my body and there were butterflies in my stomach. I didn't know if he was just doing this for comfort or if this was actually him wanting this, but either way, I had been waiting for this moment.

It started out being just innocent, but then the kiss turned deeper. As we continued, his hands went under my shirt and he quickly removed it, which cut our kissing off. Before we continued, I slipped his shirt off. He led me to his bed and one thing led to another, bringing a heat filled night.

Chapter Twenty

Lockwood

The next morning, I slowly opened my eyes, noticing the sun shining through the blinds. I looked over at my clock and saw that it was 6:30 in the morning. I had to be at work by 8:00, so I had to get up, which caused me to groan. I then noticed that Evelynn wasn't in bed with me, but I did hear commotion in the kitchen.

I replayed last night's events in my memory, and I couldn't help but smile, it was everything I had hoped for; I just wished she was in bed with me now. I thought about what led us to being in my bed and I really hoped she didn't think I used her to feel better, because that wasn't the case at all. I have been wanting what we did. I wanted to show her that I wanted her and not just in my bed, but in my life as well, and I would continue to show her in many ways, every single day.

Better get up, I thought as I sat up, wishing I didn't have to work today. I needed to find out what happened to Linda in order to save Evelynn. What was happening to Evelynn was tied to what happened to Linda. So, from here on out, this will be figured out and I will remain focused.

I got out of bed and got dressed in yesterday's clothes. I was going to shower anyway, so I would be in fresh clothes for work. I walked out of my bedroom, and I could hear sizzling from the kitchen, so I made my way there. What I found made me chuckle. I figured that she must have had earbuds in, because she was swaying her hips as she danced to whatever music she was listening to. It looked like she was making french toast. I walked up behind her and wrapped my arms around her waist, which made her jump and take her earbuds out.

"Where have you been all my life?" I asked, nuzzling into her neck.

"What do you mean?" she asked, laughing a sweet laugh and recoiling from me a little bit.

"You are making french toast... That's my favorite breakfast food," I said into her neck. She turned off the stove and turned to me.

"Guess what else we are having," she said, as she wrapped her arms around my waist, looking up at me with an amused smile. When I didn't answer, she leaned up towards me. "Bacon," she whispered, then went back down to flat feet. I smiled and kissed her; I was happy that we didn't have to struggle not to kiss anymore. Well, on my part I was struggling, because I knew she wanted me to, but I was hesitant by what everyone at the station would think. Only because she was part of the investigation.

"You definitely know the way to my heart..." I said teasingly, even though it was also true. I will admit that she was someone I was infatuated with; she was just so perfect.

"Well… you let me stay here for the night, so I thought I could do something nice for you," she said. "It's not much, but at least it's something, right?"

"You are right," I replied, letting go of her and walking over to the coffee pot. "Oh, by the way… you're not going back home until we find who killed Linda and who is doing all of this to you," I said as I grabbed a coffee mug from the cupboard, poured myself some coffee, and took a sip. I looked at Evelynn and saw the shock that was shown on her face.

"Are you sure?" she asked. "I don't want to burden you."

"If I thought you would be a burden… I wouldn't have said you were going to stay here," I said with a look. "Now… I have to get ready for work… I'll be fast, so I have time to eat the breakfast you made," I said, finishing off my coffee and setting the mug down.

"But it will get cold…" she said, looking at the french toast she made.

"I'm pretty sure it's already cold," I smirked and walked over to her, kissing the top of her head. "I'll be ready soon." I walked out of the kitchen, gathered up work clothes, and headed to the bathroom to shower.

Chapter Twenty-One
Jeremy

Jeremy: It's almost time, isn't it?

Unknown: Yes, it is… we are going to give it a week of doing nothing to make it seem like it is over.

Jeremy: But you threw a brick through her living room window, saying that she was going to die.

Unknown: Just keeping them on edge until we actually go through with our plan, but once they start losing hope and having them think that she is safe… then we will do what was planned.

Jeremy: We just need to figure out where Bradley lives because that's where she is staying. I'm guessing she will be there for a while… at least until all of this is over.

Unknown: I'll leave that up to you.

Jeremy: Alright. I'll keep you posted.

Unknown: Talk soon. Bye.

Jeremy: Bye.

Chapter Twenty-Two
Wilder

I was in one of the conference rooms at the station, looking over all the evidence we had of Linda's murder and Evelynn's incidents when I heard someone come into the room. When I turned to see who it was, I saw that it was Lockwood.

"Look who showed up," I joked, giving him a smile. "Thought you weren't going to be here for a while," I said. Lockwood came over to me and looked at the evidence we had.

"Have we figured out anything?" he asked, crossing his arms.

"Well… forensics found that the blood on Evelynn's wall was dog's blood," I explained, turning to the evidence board. "And as we already know… There were no fingerprints or footprints outside, which seems impossible, but whoever managed to do it… knew what they were doing…" I said, thinking out loud.

"You don't think it could be a cop, do you?" Lockwood asked.

"It is a possibility…" I replied, rubbing my chin. "But who here would have it out for Linda and Evelynn?" I asked, looking at him.

"That's a good question..." he said, scratching the back of his head. "What did we find out about the brick?" he asked, pointing at the picture of the brick that had the writing on it.

"The writing was just paint... I asked forensics where it came from, but they said it wasn't from here..." I thought hard and realized, "Do you think that Jeremy could be involved?" I asked. "I mean... he was friends with both of them, but what was his motive..."

"He is obviously working with someone if it is him," Lockwood mentioned. "He was in the house when the brick was thrown..." he reminded me.

"Looks like we need to have a visit with Jeremy," I said, stretching my back. "But I should either go alone or take someone else with me." I knew he wasn't going to like me not bringing him, but he was a ticking time bomb when it came to Jeremy.

"Shouldn't *I* come with you?" he asked with confusion. "This is my case too," he pointed out. I then turned to him, crossing my arms.

"After the stunt you pulled last time... I don't think it's a good idea," I said sternly. "You had it out for him the moment we first stepped into Evelynn's house."

"And that is why you are being put on suspension... with pay of course." We turned to see our chief of police.

"Are you serious!?" Lockwood asked loudly. "For how long?"

"Until this investigation is over," Chief said, placing his hands on his hips. "I let a lot of things slide, but attacking someone, I'm not gonna let fly," he said.

"He was abusing her!" Lockwood exclaimed. "And I don't have a doubt in my mind that he is a part of all of this!" he said, motioning to the board.

"If she is being abused, she should have reported it… you can't take matters into your own hands." I was surprised that he was staying so calm. Usually, they would have a yelling match. "Now… hand over your badge and gun," Chief demanded, giving Lockwood a warning look. "You're lucky I'm not terminating you for the Jaxon incident and what you have done recently."

I looked at Lockwood and I could tell he was trying hard not to let his anger get the best of him, which was good because his suspension would be lengthened.

"Gun and badge, Lockwood," Chief repeated. Lockwood stared at Chief hard, but he removed his gun from the back of his pants and took his badge from his pocket.

"See you around," I said as he placed the items on the table. He made one quick nod in my direction and headed out of the room, brushing past Chief.

"Now, you…" Chief said, putting his attention on me, "Go talk to this Jeremy guy." He then turned and walked out.

"Yes, sir," I mumbled to myself, giving one more glance at the board and then walked out of the room.

Chapter Twenty-Three

Jeremy

I had just sat down on my front steps and lit a cigarette when I saw a cop car pull up in front of the house. *Great,* I thought with annoyance. I took a drag as they got out of the car and headed up the path towards me. I couldn't help but notice that it was Wilder and one of the cops that was at Evelynn's house last night.

"No Lockwood?" I asked facetiously, taking another drag and then blowing it out with a smirk.

"He couldn't make it," Wilder responded gruffly.

Someone is in a bad mood. "Too busy banging Evelynn?" I asked nonchalantly. After everything that has happened these past two days, I stopped caring about Evelynn and what she was doing. As I see it, she isn't my responsibility anymore. Lockwood can deal with her.

"Why he isn't here is none of your concern," Wilder responded. "We came here for a little chat." He made it sound like I was a suspect, which was irritating.

"Well go on then," I said, motioning for him to continue with my hand.

"So, we stopped by the local grocery store on our way here… just to see if you really did have an alibi…" he started. "Lucky for us, someone who was working today, who usually works overnights, was covering for someone."

No doubt it was Olson. I took another drag, waiting for him to continue.

"They did say that you were working on the night of Linda's murder." A knowing smile spread across his face. "But here is the interesting part... They said you left early... right before the time of Linda's murder." He gave me a questioning look. "Why did you leave early?" he asked.

"I felt sick," I said flatly. "So, I came home and passed out in bed." I shrugged like it was no big deal. "But of course I wouldn't have an alibi for that since I live alone and all I did was sleep."

"And you didn't know about the murder since yesterday morning?" he asked.

"That's when Evie called me... so yes," I responded.

"Hm," he said with suspicion.

"If this is an interrogation..." I started to say. "Doesn't that mean I need to be taken in?" I asked standing up. "Am I being detained? I don't see you arresting me, so I can stop talking to you and just go inside," I said and did exactly that. I took out my phone and dialed a number.

"We need to hurry things up," I said on the phone. "They just came to my house and already suspect me..."

92

Chapter Twenty-Four
Evelynn

I haven't been able to relax ever since Bradley left for work. I kept thinking that whoever was doing this would come and finish me off. I would jump at every sound. I would freeze at every shadow that moved. I pretty much cleaned all of Bradley's apartment to try and keep myself distracted. I didn't have my anxiety meds since Bradley couldn't find them; even I couldn't find them, which I assume meant that this was personal. It became personal the moment Linda died, and I became the target. The strange thing was, all my other meds were still there, at least I was able to take those.

After an hour of cleaning, I felt exhausted. Usually, it wouldn't exhaust me, but after dealing with so much, it all just wore me out. I was going to lay down, but I suddenly heard the front door unlock. I watched as it slowly opened, and I started panicking a little, but then I saw Bradley walk in. I let out the breath that I didn't even know I was holding.

"You're home early…" I said to him, confused. "I thought you —" Before I could finish, he quickly came over to me and brought me into a rough kiss. It took me off guard, so I stumbled back a bit, but he held onto me so I wouldn't fall backwards. The kiss didn't stop as he led me into his bedroom, and then clothes started to be removed. I wasn't expecting this, but I let it happen. It seemed like he was upset about something, so he needed this more than I did. Once the clothes were removed, we ended up in his bed.

***

We laid there in silence as he used his fingers to draw circles on my arm, since we were snuggled up to each other. At some point, I had fallen asleep, and I didn't know how long I had been out for. The sex was rough, but I didn't care. I enjoyed it, but I wouldn't be surprised if I ended up with bruises. If he was upset for some reason, I didn't care about whatever marks I had gotten from him. We both needed the stress relief.

"You okay?" I asked him as I looked up at him.

"I'm okay now." He chuckled. "But I'm sorry about how rough I was..." he said as he placed a kiss on my forehead. "Are you okay?" he asked with concern.

"Yeah... I'm okay." I smiled at him. "A little sore, but yes...I'm okay," I reassured him. I didn't want him to think he really hurt me when he didn't. "So, what happened?" I asked softly, "You came home earlier than expected and you were upset..." He stayed silent for a second and then spoke up.

"I was put on suspension with pay until the investigation is over..." He sighed. "It's because of the incident with Jeremy… I wouldn't be surprised if he was the one to tell the chief about it," he said with annoyance. "I know Wilder wouldn't say anything, but I suppose McMillan or Anderson could have said something as well." He then groaned and looked at me. "I'm so sorry I can't help with this anymore…" I could tell he felt bad for not being able to do the investigation anymore, so I leaned up and kissed him, placing my hand on the side of his face,

"You did everything you could to keep me safe and I know you still can by being with me through the rest of this shit show," I said with a smile. "Don't be so hard on yourself for this." I saw him nod and we fell into silence again.

"Remember information for information?" he asked, breaking the silence. "Technically, I gave you what you wanted to know twice…" he said with a smirk. I gave him a confused look and he continued. "The story of why I became a cop and then my whole daughter thing," he reminded me. "So, now I get two bits of information."

"Fair enough… What do you want to know?" I asked, knowing he was going to want to know about my mental health, but I didn't know what the other thing would be, so I was a little nervous.

"Tell me about your mental health," he inquired and that made me even more nervous, because this could change how he viewed me.

"If I told you… you might see me differently… feel different about me…" I said my fears, and his response was to kiss me.

"I don't think anything you tell me will change how I feel about you," he reassured me. I took a deep breath in and slowly let it out.

"This is hard for me to talk about, but I need to tell you the back story, so you will understand how I got my diagnosis," I started to say. When I didn't get a response, I continued, "A year ago me and my dad went out to eat at Lustre Lounge. It was a celebratory dinner for me getting the new house. Well, when we were done eating… we were walking back to the car and someone grabbed me, this was at night, my dad saw me being held by someone after I was screaming for him. He tried getting me away from the guy who was holding me, but another guy grabbed him and as he was struggling against the guy… he was stabbed repeatedly…" Tears started to form in my eyes, it has been a year, but it was still fresh for me. I don't know if I'll ever be over it… I'm alone… I'll have no family ever again.

"They said he was stabbed twenty-four times… I fought so hard to get out of the grasp from the guy that was holding me, but I just couldn't get free… The guy that stabbed my dad came over to me and almost stabbed me, but a couple who came out of the restaurant yelled at us and the two guys let me go and ran off. The couple came over to see if I was okay, but I was already next to my dad… He was already dead…" Tears started falling down my face. "I didn't get a chance to say goodbye… So now, if someone I care about leaves my presence or hangs up with me when on the phone and doesn't say bye… I freak out…" I said, finishing the story.

Bradley looked down at me and wiped my tears away. "I am so sorry that that happened to you... I can't even imagine what that must have been like for you..." he murmured, tucking a loose strand of hair behind my ear.

"It's been hard to deal with, but I manage, but this brings up my mental health into play..." I said nervously. "After that, I was diagnosed with generalized anxiety, panic disorder, and PTSD... soon after it was severe depression, which branched into psychosis." I didn't want to look at him, in fear of what his reaction was. "If you want me to leave and never see me again... I understand." I was so scared he was going to have me leave, but he made me look at him,

"You're not leaving, and I don't feel anything different about you... I need to know one thing though..." He paused for a moment and then asked, "Is there a chance that you killed Linda?" It was a valid question, and I wasn't upset that he asked, but it made me a little sad.

"No," I replied flat out. "You can even ask Jeremy that I don't get aggressive. All I've dealt with is social isolation, loneliness, anxiety, lots of suicide attempts, sometimes hallucinations... there is a bit more, but nothing that would have me kill Linda," I said. "Please believe me... I don't know why 'murderer' was written on my wall, so please don't think I did it..." I begged him. He had to believe me!

"Sh, sh, sh... I believe you," he said, comforting me by tightening his hold on me. When he released me, I looked up at him. "How were you able to get through all those extreme symptoms?" he asked, looking down at me. I stayed silent for a moment, debating if I wanted to tell him what he wanted to know.

"I spent six months in the psychiatric ward after he died. Then once I was sane enough, and with Linda's persistence... I was able to leave," I said, looking away from him.

"You don't need to feel bad about that, okay?" he said, kissing my forehead. "You went through something traumatic. You *needed* help. I'm still going to be here with you... I'm not going anywhere."

I leaned up and kissed him, lingering for a moment, before looking at him again. I could tell there was something more he wanted to ask me.

I sighed. "You're itching to ask me something else... so you might as well ask it," I said to him, I just wanted to get all the information out so I can get out of being suspected of killing Linda.

"When the police were there... Wouldn't you have heard the sirens or at least seen the flashing lights?" he asked me.

"I was in my room working on my deadline for my editor. I was so far behind that I needed to focus on it. As you saw, my bedroom is in the back of the house, so I couldn't see the lights. I also had earbuds in with the music blasting, so the sirens weren't something I could hear," I explained. "I know you just said that you believe me for not killing Linda and I can't stress it enough that I didn't, but I don't really have an alibi…"

"Did you submit your edits to your editor that night?" he asked, with his cop curiosity.

"Yes, I did actually, but I can't really show that to you when I don't have my laptop anymore," I said, before I sighed.

"Well, let's get my laptop charged and you can show me that you did that, that night," he said with a smile. "More evidence of you not killing Linda, will help a lot to clear your name."

Chapter Twenty-Five

Lockwood

Evelynn became very vulnerable with me, and I appreciated that she had told me, but I still needed to know one more thing. "What happened at Jeremy's that made you scared of being there?" I asked her. With her now being silent, I knew I wouldn't like what she was going to tell me.

"He nearly killed me in there," she started to say. "I made him really mad at me and he beat me so badly that I ended up in the hospital." She didn't look at me as she told me this. I listened intently as she told me her story and my blood started to boil.

***

I was sitting on Jeremy's bed, while he paced back and forth in his room, ranting and raving about things at work. He had been drinking his alcohol of choice, whiskey. He was now on his fifth glass, which he had just downed. With the fact of him swaying and slurring his words, I knew he had enough.

"Jeremy... I think you need to be done drinking for the night," I said to him, resting my head against his wall. He stopped pacing and turned to me; with the face I feared.

"*Are you cutting me off?*" *he snapped, grabbing the almost empty bottle.* "*There is more that needs to be drunk,*" *he said, filling the rest of the liquid in his glass. All the way to the rim. I scooted off his bed and stood up, refusing to look at him.*

"*I think I'm going to go…*" *I said as I headed to the bedroom door, but I didn't get far because Jeremy grabbed my arm to stop me. He then threw me up against his wall and held my neck, making it hard to breathe.*

"*You do **not** tell me what to do!*" *he growled, then threw me onto the floor. Before I could make my escape, he climbed on top of me and backhanded me across the face. I tried fighting him, but he grabbed my wrists and put my arms above my head.*

"*Jeremy! Stop!*" *I yelled as I continued to fight. He lied to me. He said he would never do this.*

"*You **really** think you can tell me what to do!?*" *he yelled as he started, unbuttoning my jeans.*

"*No!*" *I yelled and without even thinking, I kneed him in the crotch, which caused him to let go of me. I tried getting up to get out of there, but he grabbed me by the leg and brought me closer to him.*

"***You** are **not** going anywhere,*" *he said as he got on top of me again. He then punched me across the face.* "*You do **not** attack me!*" *He threw another punch to my face.*

"*Stop, Jeremy!*" *I said, as I started to cry.*

"Shut up!" Another blow to the face. I could feel that my nose broke and it was a sickening crack. He then stood up and kicked me in the stomach. "You think you can reject me?" he growled, kicking me again. At this point, I couldn't say anything, but what was the point? He wasn't going to stop. I was gasping for breath from him kicking me in the stomach, but another blow came. "You are **mine** to do what I want with... and **no one** will save you!" The next kick was to the face and then he got on top of me again.

He wrapped his hands around my neck and started to squeeze tight, cutting off my airway. I grabbed at his hands, but I was too weak to even attempt to get out of it, but I had to try and that earned me another blow to the face. "Do **not** fight me, you deserve this!"

Darkness was appearing around the corners of my eyes, and I just knew I was going to die. Soon, my body went limp, and blackness took over.

***

Once she finished her story, it threw me over the edge. I got up quickly and then started to get dressed. I would not let him get away with that. If it got me fired, at this point, I didn't give a shit. I'll do what I did to Jaxon and what Jeremy did to her.

"What are you doing?" she asked me frantically as she sat up.

"Paying a little visit to Jeremy," I growled. I would show him no mercy.

"No! Please, don't!" she begged me, as she got out of bed and quickly got dressed. "Don't go! I need you here!" she exclaimed. I went over to her and brought her into a kiss, lingering for a moment before pulling away.

"I won't be gone long," I said and then walked out of the bedroom, with her trailing behind me continuing to beg me not to leave. I wasn't listening though. I reached under the dining room table and grabbed my personal gun.

"Bradley…" I heard her say my name, but as soon as my shoes were on, I was out the door. Nothing was going to stop me from getting to Jeremy.

Chapter Twenty-Six

Evelynn

I couldn't stop him. I needed him here and he left. He was going to 'take care' of Jeremy and I didn't know what would happen. I hadn't gotten a new phone yet, and I don't even think he brought his phone with him, so there was no way of contacting him. I couldn't go after him because the only car that was here for us to use was my car. I didn't know what to do. I don't even know what I *could* do. I was pacing the living room, trying not to have a panic attack, because I still didn't have my anxiety meds. There was so much that could go wrong with Bradley doing this, but I needed to stop him, but I didn't know how. I was helpless.

Suddenly there was a knock on the door. I turned and stared at it, not knowing if I should answer it. Then there was another knock. Maybe it was Detective Wilder? A neighbor that may need help? Making up my mind, I walked over to the door and looked into the peephole. I sighed in relief when I saw that it was Detective Wilder. I immediately opened the door and didn't give him a chance to talk.

"Bradley is going after Jeremy!" I said hurriedly.

"What?" Wilder bellowed. "What happened?" he asked me.

"We were talking, and he asked me why I was afraid of going to Jeremy's house," I began. "I told him the reason and now I think he is going to kill Jeremy!" I exclaimed, as I was getting my shoes on. "So, we have to go!"

"Alright. Let's go," Wilder said and we were out the door, running down the hall. When we got to his police cruiser, we quickly got in. Wilder turned on his lights and siren, and then he sped out of the apartment complex and down the road. I had never been in a cop car before, so I was looking around at all the equipment. It all looked so complicated.

"So, what was the reason?" Wilder asked loudly. I knew he was angry and, in a panic, while I was just in a panic.

"Jeremy, one time, almost killed me," I said.

"And you didn't tell the police?" he asked.

"I couldn't! He told them lies about what happened!" I yelled. "I was scared of what he would have done if I told them what really happened. He has done horrible things to me, Detective," I explained. "So much worse than a quick death…"

"Does Lockwood know that?" he asked, probably hoping not to hear what he was thinking.

"No," I responded as he turned his sirens and lights off. I looked out the window and saw we were close to our destination. There was a chance that Jeremy could be dead by now.

We soon arrived at Jeremy's house and Wilder cut the engine. I could see my car parked in front of us. Right now, the fear I was feeling was not because I was here, it was because I didn't know what I would find.

"First off..." Wilder started to say. "Once all of this is over... you're getting a restraining order against Jeremy," he ordered. I looked at the clock and was surprised to see that it was 7:05 pm. "Secondly... you need to stay here... I don't know what we are dealing with," he said, but I wasn't going to just stay in the car.

"No! I'm coming—" Suddenly there was a gunshot. I looked towards the house and quickly got out.

"Evelynn!" Wilder called out, but I was already running to the house. When I got there, I threw open the door, and when I entered, I saw Jeremy on the floor. Luckily, unhurt, but then I saw Bradley pointing his gun at him. Wilder came up behind me and was now pointing his gun at Bradley.

"Lockwood... you need to put the gun down," he warned Bradley. "Do not make me pull this trigger..."

"He is not going to get away with what he did to Evelynn!" Bradley barked angrily.

"Bradley... please don't..." I pleaded, stepping a little closer to him. "I know what he did was terrible, but killing him isn't the answer..." I took a few more steps. I just needed to get to him, but I had to be slow about it, like he was with me.

"Evelynn!" Wilder hissed, but I wasn't listening to him.

"You better listen to her," Jeremy said with a smirk on his face, he didn't seem scared at all. "This could end badly for you."

"Shut up, Jeremy!" I snapped and turned my attention back to Bradley. I was so close to getting to him.

"What would you do in this situation then? What would you do if it was me who almost died by his hands?" Bradley asked, getting ready to pull the trigger.

"Not this…" I responded, stepping in front of him, so the gun was now pointed at me. If I was in the way, I knew he wouldn't shoot.

"What are you doing!?" Wilder shouted, but I held my hand out towards him, signaling for him to be quiet.

"Move…" Bradley growled, but he knew I wasn't going to. Instead, I took a step closer and placed the gun on my forehead, he had no choice but to lower his gun or shoot me.

"You either drop your gun or kill me," I said sternly, as I looked into his horrified eyes. "If you did this… you will be locked up for the rest of your life and I will not live a life that doesn't have you in it."

Chapter Twenty-Seven

Lockwood

I instantly dropped the gun and pulled her into a deepened kiss, holding the sides of her face. What was I thinking? I couldn't leave her, she needed me, like I needed her. When I released the kiss, I placed my forehead on hers.

"Let's go home," I said softly. I didn't want to mention this to her at the time, because I didn't want her to freak out, but I loved her, since after the conversation we had in her bedroom when we first met. I guess you could call it love at first sight. I will eventually tell her that I love her but now wasn't a good time.

"Well, aren't you two a sight for sore eyes," Jeremey said sarcastically, as he stood up and stupidly said, "Taking her from me was your last mistake…" Which caused me to smirk. Jeremy had a confused look on his face, until Wilder walked over to him and forcefully put Jeremy's hands behind his back, "What are you—"

"You are under arrest for threatening a police officer…" Then Wilder started reading off his Miranda rights, while Jeremy argued about how ridiculous this was and that his lawyer would come and take care of this.

Relief was on Evelynn's face as Jeremy was pushed out the front door, and I was happy that she wouldn't have to deal with his abuse anymore, along with everything else that had happened to her these past few days, if it was him. It had to be him. There was no one else that she knew that I knew of, that could have done all of this. Honestly, I was surprised Wilder didn't arrest me for what I just did, but I am grateful that he didn't.

I turned to Evelynn and wrapped an arm around her. "Let's go," I said as I kissed her on top of her head, grabbed my gun, and led her out.

"You know the captain will find out about this…" Wilder said as he approached us. "It won't be by me, but jackass probably will say something," he mentioned, looking towards his cruiser with Jeremy inside. "Won't be surprised if you get fired, but hopefully not," he sighed, turning back to us. "Go home." He then went back to his cruiser.

I brought Evelynn to her car and helped her into the passenger side. "You're going to hurt your shoulder more if you keep driving," she teased me as I put her seatbelt on.

"Well, there would be one other thing I would have to stop if you don't want me to hurt more," I said, with a wink. When I saw her face turn red, I couldn't help but laugh and then shut the car door. She didn't know that that's what was going to happen once we got home. The way she handled me, and the situation, wasn't something that I have ever had happened before. No female would have approached me when I was in a rage, especially with a gun in my hand. It just showed that she actually *did* care about me. When she said, '*If you did this… you will be locked up for the rest of your life and I will not live a life that doesn't have you in it.'* I couldn't help the way I reacted. That statement just overwhelmed me with so many emotions and that was all I could do to show her how much that meant to me.

I got into the driver's seat and started the car, but before driving off, I looked at her. "Thank you for getting me through that… I would have killed him if you didn't show up," I said, feeling resentful towards myself. I never wanted her to see me like that. I had a therapy appointment coming up, so I would work through it with my therapist. I was given that order after the Jaxon incident.

"I just couldn't bear the thought of you not being here with me," she replied, looking down at her hands. "But you are going to get in trouble with your job, right?" she asked sadly. "I didn't want this for you when I told you everything."

"Hey…" I started saying as I turned her head towards me, so she could focus on me. "This isn't your fault. I have never been able to control my anger," I explained to her. "So, this is on me, not you, okay?" I reassured her. I couldn't let her believe that it was her fault because it was in no way hers. When I got a nod from her, I leaned over and kissed her. "Everything is going to be okay…" I reassured her, as I moved away from her. "Now for real this time… Let's go home," I said and then drove off down the street.

Chapter Twenty-Eight
Wilder

What was Lockwood thinking? If he had killed Jeremy, he would have ruined his life. It was already fucked if the captain found out, which I believe he will because Jeremy will tell him about it. What did Evelynn say that made Lockwood's anger so bad that he was willing to commit murder? I thought for a moment when it dawned on me. She said that Jeremy almost killed her, but why? That would be something to ask Evelynn when the time comes.

"I'll make sure you and him get fired and not be able to work in any police stat—" Jeremy started to say angrily, but I didn't let him finish,

"Shut it, Andrews!" I snapped, glaring at him through the rearview mirror. I saw him scowl and leaned back again.

"You won't be able to hold me..." Jeremy muttered. I just rolled my eyes and continued to drive, until we got to the station. Once parked, I got out of the car and opened the door on the side that Jeremy was in.

"Here we go," I said, pulling Jeremy out of the car roughly. "From here on out... you're going to want to keep your mouth shut," I suggested. "You will be around a lot of cops." I smirked, as I led him into the station.

Chapter Twenty-Nine

Evelynn

A week had gone by with no incidents. Maybe it was Jeremy the whole time and maybe that's why nothing has happened? It has been a sense of relief, but I still couldn't help being worried. Bradley hasn't let me go home yet, because I think he was worried too.

I slept in today, because I felt like I really needed sleep. I got out of bed, stretched, and then went to the bathroom. When I was done, I headed into the kitchen, hoping Bradley made coffee before he left for his appointment. He had woken me up for a moment to say he was leaving, but then I instantly fell asleep right as he left the room.

As I entered the kitchen, I stopped short; there on the counter was a stargazer lily, which was my favorite flower, and next to it was a note. I slowly walked towards the note and picked it up.

I'm coming for you...

I dropped the note, ran back into the bedroom, and grabbed my phone. We got it for me during the week, along with a new laptop. I needed to know if Jeremy was let go of police custody. I quickly pushed the call button on Wilder's contact and listened to it ring. After the third ring, he picked up.

"Evelynn... What's going on?" he asked, alarmed. I didn't usually call him unless it was important.

"Is Jeremy still in custody?" I asked in a panic, reaching for my anxiety meds. I was able to get it filled, since it was time for a refill anyway. I took one of the pills and swallowed it with water.

"Yeah, he is..." Wilder answered. "He is in a holding cell right now..." He was starting to sound concerned. "What happened, Evelynn?" he asked.

"I woke up just a little bit ago. Bradley is at an appointment, but I came into the kitchen... and on the counter was my favorite flower and a note saying 'I'm coming for you...'" I explained, as I sat on the bed. There was a moment of silence, then Wilder spoke up again,

"Alright... I'll be there soon," he said. "Try and get a hold of Lockwood," he instructed.

"Okay, I will. Bye," I said, fidgeting with my pajama pants.

"It will be okay. Bye."

I hung up the call and quickly called Bradley, but it kept ringing until the voicemail kicked in. As soon as I heard the beep, I started rambling. "I'm so scared... Bradley... it's not over and Wilder said that Jeremy is still in custody," I stood up and started pacing. "My favorite flower was on the counter and a note… please come home as fast as you can…" I then hung up the phone and put it on the bed. *I hope he gets home soon*, I thought.

    I sat there until the meds kicked in, waiting to feel completely calm, but it was short lived. There was a knock on the door.

Chapter Thirty

Lockwood

As I was leaving my therapy session, I noticed that Evelynn had called. When I left the building, I listened to her voicemail and instantly hung up, sprinting to Evelynn's car. When I got in, I called her, but there was no answer. I tried again but got the same outcome. I decided to call Wilder because he would get there before me.

"Lockwood... Did you talk to—" I didn't let him finish; I was too much in a panic.

"She didn't answer her phone when I called her twice..." I said as I turned the ignition on and sped out of the parking lot and onto the street. "Do you think you could head over there?" I asked, taking a sharp right.

"Already on my way," he said, "She called me too."

"Please hurry." I then hung up the call. I was going as fast as I could, without getting pulled over. I tried calling Evelynn again, but I still got no answer.

"FUCK!"

Chapter Thirty-One
Evelynn

I stood there not being able to move, not until I heard a second knock. I sighed in relief when I realized that it could be Wilder. I walked into the living room and went up to the door. I looked through the peephole, but didn't see anyone. *That's strange,* I thought, moving away from the door. I didn't get very far as I walked away, because there was, once again, a knock on the door.

I walked back to the door, placing my hand on the doorknob. I took a deep breath in, blew it out, and opened the door, but there was no one there. I was about to shut it again, but suddenly a gun was pointed at me. I stepped backwards, as someone came out from the side of the doorway.

At first, I didn't register who it was, but when I realized it, I was in complete shock.

"Linda?"

Chapter Thirty-Two

Linda

"Surprise," I said with a cheeky smile. I was *so* much looking forward to this moment. It took a lot of planning. Everything I did took planning. I walked into the apartment and shut the door, locking it, without moving the gun away from Evelynn. "How has everything been going?" I asked her with a smirk. "Enjoying everything these past two weeks?" I was just toying with her and the look of shock and fear only made this more exciting.

"How... How are you..." She was stumbling through her words, so I decided to help her out.

"How am I alive?" I said, finishing her thought. "I faked my own death... that way I could pin it on *you*," I explained. "But you wouldn't have gone to jail... just the psych ward. I wanted everyone to think that you had gone crazy so they would just lock you up and good luck getting out again..." I said. "See... it started out with the message on your mirror... that was a tricky thing to do..." I went and leaned on the wall that was behind me. We suddenly heard her phone start ringing. She couldn't do anything though, since I had a gun pointed at her. When the phone stopped ringing, it didn't take long for it to ring again.

"Wow, that's annoying..." I said annoyed. "Anyways..." I started to talk again, "Where was I? Oh, yeah! So, the next step was your phone, which was easier to do... I was already in the house, so it was a quick in and out."

"Why?" Evelynn whimpered.

Pathetic, I thought. "I went on a jealous rage." I shrugged. "So, I picked up the ante... I was going to keep things small and gradually get bigger, but you started getting friendly with Detective Lockwood..."

"Why does that matter?" she asked. "Why would you be jealous?" she asked. Then I noticed that she was trying to move towards the kitchen.

"I wouldn't do that if I were you..." I said, cocking the gun. "Unless you want to get shot," I threatened, which caused her to stop. I had a silencer on the gun, so no one would hear if I pulled the trigger. I motioned for her to go back to where she was with my gun. She listened and went back into the living room where she was before. "Now, I'll answer your question." I paused for a second. "You didn't realize what all I have done for you? I'm not surprised, since you're so spacey..." I sighed. "It's because I have always loved you," I said quietly, but loud enough so she could still hear me.

"So, you wanted me to end up in the psych ward?" she asked with confusion.

"It was the only way to prevent you from being with anyone else... Then the detective came into the picture, so out of jealousy... I destroyed your house and wrote murderer on the wall... just to speed things up. Then you guys suspected Jeremy... which was our plan, along with getting him arrested," I said nonchalantly. "But don't worry... he will be set free... What he said wasn't totally a threat," I explained with a smirk.

"Evelynn!" We heard Detective Lockwood call in the distance.

"Looks like your knight and shining armor is here," I said as I un-cocked the gun and put it in the back of my pants. I then dug in my pocket and pulled out a switchblade. "Now... be a good girl and don't run."

Chapter Thirty-Three

Lockwood

I had gotten there as fast as I could, I just hoped that Wilder was already here. I didn't see his cruiser though. *Shit,* I thought, just stopping the car in front of the apartment building. There was no way I was taking the time to park. I got out of Evelynn's car and was about to run inside, but then I saw the flash of red and blue lights coming into the parking lot. The cruiser stopped next to the car and Wilder quickly got out.

"Sorry I wasn't here sooner… there were assholes that wouldn't get out of my way," he explained with annoyance.

"It doesn't matter now that you're here, so let's get inside!" I said loudly, as I started running towards the door, with Wilder following close behind. I swung open the door, just as someone walked out of the building, and ran up the stairs, two at a time, until we came to the second floor. Both Wilder and I had our guns in our hands as we ran down the hall. "Evelynn!" I called out, letting her know that I was coming.

Once we got to my door, I tried opening it, but it was locked. I started searching for my keys, but I couldn't find them… "Shit. I think I left my keys in the car."

Wilder then smirked. "Guess we will have to open it the cop way..." He lifted his leg and kicked the door in. When we entered my apartment, I saw the situation and it made my heart sink. Evelynn was being held in place, with a switchblade knife to her throat, then I saw who was behind her. Wilder and I both had our guns pointed in that direction. We were shocked by who it was, but we needed to stay level-headed.

"Miss Walker... I need you to drop the knife and let Evelynn go," Wilder instructed sternly. I was aiming right at Linda's head, even though she was blocked by Evelynn.

Just one move... just one... I thought, trying to be patient, but it was so damn hard because it was Evelynn who was being threatened.

"Kayne... seriously? You don't need to be all formal. I mean... we were fuck buddies for a while... then you caught feelings, so it just didn't work out between us," Linda said, a little annoyed. "Anyways... It's really *his* fault that we are in this situation," Linda said, pointing the knife at me and then putting it back against Evelynn's neck.

"How is it my fault?" I asked, puzzled. *What could I have possibly done?* I was shocked to hear about Wilder and Linda, but that didn't matter at this point.

"You ruined my plan and stole her from me!" Linda yelled, pressing the knife harder against Evelynn's neck, which caused a bit of blood to fall down her neck, "I have loved her since I had gotten to know her, but then you came waltzing in and she wanted to be with you!" Linda exclaimed. "I was going to have her put in the psych ward so I could have her to myself…" She then leaned forward, close to Evelynn's neck, and placed a kiss on it. I saw Evelynn flinch away, but Linda had her firmly in her grasp.

"Last warning, Miss Walker… drop the knife and let her go…" Wilder warned. Wilder would not hesitate to pull the trigger if he had to. Linda looked at Wilder, rolling her eyes, and then to me.

"Looks like if I can't have her… then neither can *you*…" She quickly slashed Evelynn's neck, but didn't make it to the middle, because Wilder shot Linda in the head, instantly killing her. Evelynn fell to the ground, while blood pooled out of her neck. I ran over to her and fell to the floor, taking her in my arms, and putting pressure on her neck. Wilder was already calling for an ambulance.

"You're going to be okay… stay with me, baby… I need you…" I begged repeatedly. She was slipping towards death, and I didn't know what to do. I had put pressure on the wound to slow the bleeding, but it just continued gushing out. I pulled her closer to me and started to cry. Her breathing had started getting shallow. "Please… stay with me…" I continued to beg. She just couldn't die. She had no idea how much I needed her. How much she meant to me. I leaned towards her ear and whispered,

"I love you."

Chapter Thirty-Four

Evelynn

It's weird having this feeling of dying. You don't really feel the pain after a bit, because you're in shock. I knew I was going to die. I didn't want to, but I knew I was dying.

I could hear Bradley beg me to stay, but I didn't know if I would be able to. Fighting against it just made me so tired. I didn't know how much more fight my body could handle.

"I love you."

I heard those words, and I knew I had to keep fighting, but it was just so hard. I would keep fighting until I couldn't anymore, but my body was starting to shut down. I heard sirens in the distance, but I feared that they would be too late. I opened my eyes as much as I could, slowly lifting my hand to touch his face and I knew what I needed to say before the end.

"I love you, too."

Then everything went black.

Epilogue

Lockwood

It's been a year since Evelynn died. It was hard to deal with while she was lying in my arms, and I could tell how much she was trying to fight death, but life has a funny way of showing itself.

I was sitting on the deck of a cabin that I owned, just watching the water of the lake I lived by, when I heard the door open and close.

"I was wondering where you went," Evelynn said as she sat on my lap. "I woke up and you weren't there," she said, laying her head on my shoulder.

Death was no match for her, she continued fighting until she died, but the paramedics were able to bring her back. They had to do a transfusion to keep her alive, but she had died two more times before she was stable and there were no more incidents.

She had lived.

About The Author

Kelsie was born and raised in Minnesota. She has three children, three cats, and has been married for eight years. She decided to pursue her writing career because she wanted to follow in her grandpa's footsteps. She, of course, always was interested in writing, ever since her days in school. This book is her first ever published novel.

Photo Credit: Killer Photography

Made in the USA
Monee, IL
19 July 2025